1888 DIAL INDIA

ANUVAB PAL

1888 DIAL INDIA

EBURY PRESS

An imprint of Penguin Random House

EBURY PRESS

USA | Canada | UK | Ireland | Australia
New Zealand | India | South Africa | China | Singapore

Ebury Press is part of the Penguin Random House group of companies whose addresses can be found at global.penguinrandomhouse.com

Published by Penguin Random House India Pvt. Ltd
4th Floor, Capital Tower 1, MG Road,
Gurugram 122 002, Haryana, India

Penguin Random House India

First published by Random House India 2011

10 9 8 7 6 5 4 3 2

ISBN 9788184001587

Typeset in Bembo Std by Eleven Arts

Printed at Manipal Technologies Limited, India

www.penguin.co.in

FSC www.fsc.org MIX Paper | Supporting responsible forestry FSC® C043100

This is a legitimate digitally printed version of the book and therefore might not have certain extra finishing on the cover.

To my Dad,

For teaching me that pursuing an impossible dream is the only life worth living.

And for being the cleverest man I know.

1888 Dial India premiered as a stage play on July 5, 2009 at St. Andrews Auditorium in Mumbai, presented by Raell Padamsee's Ace Productions.

The original cast featured:

Kunaal Roy Kapur,
Sophie Chaudhary,
Ashwin Mushran,
Ratnabali Bhattacharjee,
Faezeh Jalili,
Siddharth Kumar,
Prerna Chawla,
Pallavi Sharda,
Hazel Keech, and
Anand Tiwari

At the time of this publication, the play had finished twenty shows and continues to be staged across India.

'Since 1991, after the country's economic freedom
a new Indian businessman has emerged.
Confident, ambitious, relentless, free of class, caste
and hierarchy. Their huge dreams are building
what is being called "The New India".'

IMF/World Bank Report, 2006

Contents

Why am I writing a memoir?

Look at the past.

What were we to the West? Beggars. City of Joy, fucking rikshaw-pulling untouchables? They loved Satyajit Ray showing cute orphans fighting over a handful of rice. In Indiana Jones, we're getting excited eating monkey brains. Plague. That's what they thought of India. Burning widows. Sewage. Famine. Rats. And when we were not living in a drain, we were waiting for IMF aid. Worse than the blacks because at least the whites or pop stars could sing 'We are the World' and send money to Africa. We were just a piece of shit on the world map, sitting in our ambassador cars staring at a leper begging for a devaluing rupee. See, back then I couldn't say much because of two things...I was small and foreigners were right.

But today, look at what we're doing. Just look outside. The Mumbai skyline is a sea of cranes building glass towers and glass malls, trying to make New York look like my asshole. That was a joke. Yes, we're still poor and our roads are shit but we have fucking confidence. When I land in London, I'm not some Bangladeshi immigrant stirring a pot of Makhni, I'm Arun fucking Gupta, self-made millionaire, with a three-star hotel reservation on Gloucester Road, breakfast included—about to hire four of your whites for sales. I have confidence to stand in front here, wearing this Italian clothing, genuine 73 percent leather, and say, 'Madam, if I start a new business, a billion people are my market.'

And a billion people are thinking like that. IPL, Airtel, Reliance, Infosys, TATA, PVR…thousands of thinkers, not as smart as me but still…building only on confidence that we want a bigger, better fucking country. A place where we can wipe off that piece of shit and stand up to say to the world, we are Indians, and you will say, pay attention, these Indians now matter. That's the real City of Joy. The rickshaw puller is sitting in the rickshaw now.

People say, Arun, how did you get such big balls to take so many chances? How are you such a visionary for the new India? And I say, it came this way. My balls were always like this. Ever since I saw my government family dying when the government pensions couldn't pay for government hospitals because they didn't know how to make some noise. I decided, I will make noise. The new India will make some noise. No apologies. No 'hello, sir, I'll wipe your ass, sir, make me a member of your Gymkhana Club, sir', none of that homo British shit. Just big dreams. Just big cash. No saying 'love all Indians.' When I'm old, my government, my children will take care of me. Fuck that, only I love me. And everyone who is out there looking for gold, are only looking out for themselves. It's the Wild West. In the East. That's the new India.

You may ask, what is the story of *1888 Dial India*? How did it all happen and how did you become what you became? Yes, most of the stuff is now legendary and all over the left-hand column of the last page of the *Economic Times*, June 23, 2008, but that's only media hype. There's a bigger story. I will tell it. Like the rise of Facebook, Coca Cola, Twitter, Microsoft, and the Reserve Bank of India, there are humble beginnings, heroic acts, jealous rivals, epic battles. Ending with me still here so you can guess who won.

Today I drive a Skoda whose installments are no longer overdue. Aparna from the *Economic Times* doesn't use the word 'criminal' and me in the same article anymore. I live in an India where I can drink Costa. A British multinational is grovelling for market share of India's seven hundred million urban middle class. I predicted this in 2003. The architects who will build my new office for my new business idea are among the best in the USA, but I will make them wait with my Bengali secretary. I have always wanted to hire a Bengali secretary with an MA. Ideally in English Literature. I won't go into why. It has something to do with Aparna Sen getting wet.

For all these reasons, I need to write a memoir.

Arun Gupta
May, 2010

Not so humble beginnings

Like all great things in history, it was an accident.

I remember it was the monsoons, because another Air India flight had just flown into a tree in the south somewhere and a different Congress MP was in a different jail for a different corruption scandal.

My last business venture, a call centre, was wrapping up. No, not folding, taking a break, like they do in cricket after every ball.

See, the thing is, it's very easy for people to say that the business venture was failing. That's what people do—say—'See he failed'. People are like that. Dictionaries define people as a group of persons but that's not how Arun Gupta defines them. He sees people as a group of assholes who don't have the balls to give up being servants for Marwaris and live in their company flat having their life sucked out of them just like their monthly TDS. And to those 'people', I say, 'I passed'. No, I didn't pass in ICSE or ISC or BCom (passing those don't matter. If you're studying for those and reading this, stop studying right now and finish this first).

I'm not going to get into why I wasn't allowed to finish my ISC for that alu bomb I threw at Reverend Suarez or why my BCom final centre entry pass said 'Thane' instead of 'Pune' (fuck you typists of India. Thank God, you're finished by Lenovo).

Those things are not the point in this kind of passing. This passing is far more important. No, I'm not going to say 'the classroom of life' or some such shit you read in US self-help books. Hate those things. They are business obstacles for my new business venture. You'll find out why soon. No, I mean passing from one business to another. Upward mobility. Advancing. In this case, I was shifting from one room to the next, so sideways mobility. Whatever. Mobility, that's the main thing. Moving. That's how economies grow, when people pass from business to business. Things start in garages, end up in skyscrapers. Hong Kong wasn't built by a bunch of Chinese billionaires sitting in one place. That's the journey I was on. In most cases, people start a business, leave it thriving to their children and move to the next. In my case, I was closing a business and then starting a new one. Some cynical young MBA fuckers reading this will say, 'Oh but that's not upward mobility. That's just tax evading'. You know what I say to you, come check my Form 16. Every exit does not have to leave something behind just because you've exited it. A famous person once said, 'every exit can be an entrance to somewhere else.' That's me.

It was a call centre to repair American home appliances on the phone. Mostly toasters, phones, TVs, air conditioners. © I have trademarked the idea so if any fucker reading this tries to copy it, just know, it is a brilliant idea and I will get back to it someday and if I see you competing with me, send me your address for the royalty notice.

Like destiny or George Michael's career, it was heading for a huge success, I thought, but the main problem with these American appliance-user fuckers was that they preferred calling the actual company that sold them the product. And those bastards, like LG, Samsung, Carrier, already had outsourced lines in India.

We got fucked a little bit.

My team, which was Sudhir, my employee, couldn't help anyone and ended up destroying eleven televisions, five microwaves, and setting two GE dishwashers on fire. But it was not all his fault. I should have bought the online training appliance module instead of downloading only half of it from Bit Torrent. But give me a break, deude, as my hero Ricky Martin often said after he became openly homo. I mean, even Bill Gates dropped out of college.

Anyways (common US phrase), if I had downloaded the whole thing, maybe Sudhir's last call wouldn't have blown up the Wyoming Public Library based on his advice on what to do with their central heating. But you know what, life, as great men once said, is all a game of chance. I feel that way about outsourced home appliance customer service. One of the first rules I learnt in that business is that if you have one employee and then you fire them, productivity decreases. Always remember that.

On the flip side, however, if I hadn't gotten that asset-seizing order from the Wyoming Governor to the Indian Ambassador in Washington to the Vile Parle police station, I wouldn't be taking a break from home appliances and I wouldn't have come up with *1888 Dial India*. They said Einstein came up with the atom bomb while playing with a ball in a bathtub. This was like that. Only bigger.

I was about four minutes from disconnecting our 1-800 bridge line. Those fuckers were charging me too much so I decided to ride on a British Telecom line actually belonging to Larsen and Toubro. They never found out, except sometimes they would have conference calls with their board of directors and get confused as to why some old lady in Minnesota was talking about baking ovens. So, there I was, four minutes from disconnection, when suddenly, the phone rang.

It confused me.

Everyone knew we were not operational thanks to that Wall Street Journal story. I don't want to go into that right now.

It was a woman's voice.

'I'm in Chicago. I'm going to jump off the Sears Tower.'

I didn't know what to say. 'Okay, madam.' Agreeing seemed to be better than disagreeing, that's what Britain and America did in the two world wars.

'You don't have anything else to say?'

Now she stumped me. 'Madam, don't do it.' Under the circumstances, it seemed like a brilliant response. Like Vikram Pandit saving Citigroup.

'Fuck you.'

Then I just heard 'Aaaaaaaaaaahhh…', like she was on a roller coaster but not enjoying it.

Sometime later, I found out that she, this Chicago, was an Options Trader. From the voice, I could tell she was generally nervous and I assumed she was about to kill herself. Also, 'I am going to jump off Sears Tower', was a clue. It's a pretty tall building over there. It's got no class like the Burj, but still. The main thing was that she had run out of options. Later, I told that joke to my new employees—options trader, no options—but nobody laughed.

This is the problem with Indians. No sense of humour.

You might be wondering what happened to her. She died. It was very sad. And a simple communication error.

She was looking for a different 1-800. Clearly some personal helpline. Not Larsen and Toubro and not appliance repair. And accidentally called me. Like Einstein's bathtub moment (a lot of people don't know this but when he discovered the nuclear bomb in his bathtub, he said, 'Eureka', and jumped out), I had a Eureka moment.

I remember it was raining again and that leak had extended to the bedroom. Also, Bhola, my cook, was naked in the kitchen for some reason.

I said Eureka. If the US can call us to ask to repair an Epson printer, why not life?

Chicago had called us but I couldn't repair her. But maybe it's bigger than that. There are others over there, in the US, like her, on the verge of death, broken, with no repair.

That's where it all began.

And that's how it usually does. With one four-letter word.

Idea.

There are things more important in life than start-up capital. Wrong.

Sarah Coverly from General Pacific Capital is very ugly. But she did go to Wharton Business School with Anil Ambani, a fact she keeps fucking telling me at various Indo-US business forums and I almost want to tell her, 'I know he was in your class'. Sanjay Dutt was in my class but I don't go around pushing that in people's faces. Anyways, whatever.

It was June, I think, but could be January, I don't know. She had seed-funded a call-centre venture which started out as reading aloud financial statements for blind Iowa pensioners but later tried to diversify into sex chat lines. You may remember 1-800-Blow Jobs. There was an article in the *Hindustan Times* about how the CBI raided my office and.... Anyway, I don't want to talk about blow jobs in my memoir. Great business books don't have that sort of thing. Lee Iacocca's book doesn't have it.

I met Sarah randomly again on a Lufthansa flight. She was coming here to check up on some money they had invested in Harishpur Chini, which is BSE listed or whatever. I told her that I know Gopal. Harishpur is his. He owns it. I mean, it's a public limited company with shareholders and a CEO and a board of directors and all that nonsense circus one does in India to make a company look like it's more than one person even though it's basically him. That's the thing about Indian business, it can be dealing with hundreds of crores but everything is always down to one man. In Harishpur's case, Gopal. Gopal's a bloody thief who spends all his time playing squash at Bombay Gymkhana, and then later with Suresh's wife…whatever, I'm not petty. I told her about my new business venture, and asked her to meet me. She had thirty minutes before her flight back to New York, and she came around to the office.

Thing is, we had to vacate that DBS Andheri business centre because the DBS people kept saying they didn't get my wire transfers. Doing business in India is a pain, you know, because people are such cheats. So when I say Sarah came to the office, she came home, which at the time was a home-office really. But she didn't know that, and she didn't need to. Or that Antara had left me for a while. In this day and age, information is power. You may not have heard this phrase but it's something we use in business a lot. Some information is on a 'strictly need-to-know basis'. What that means is, nobody needs to know. Information is knowing. That's another key takeaway. Takeaway is an American business phrase. When you do business with them, which people reading this book will get inspired and do, using the word 'takeaway' in meetings is also a takeaway.

Before she got there, I threw away all the pizza boxes and those damn letters Citibank and HSBC kept sending me. Some reminder for payment, some other nonsense purchase cufflinks rubbish. These guys should be banned. I mean how does anyone get any work done if these banks keep calling and saying some little credit card payment is overdue a year. Continuous telemarketing.

First of all, let me clarify the rumour about my house—Prajakat Housing Society is not a redeveloped slum. *Prakajat* Housing Society in Mulund or some other garbage dump is the place where the gangster was arrested for the shootout. This is Andheri. That stuff doesn't happen here. Okay, yes, last week three RAW agents did knock on my door asking if I knew a Mohammed Khan alias Halu but that's a one-off thing. He had probably left some stuff behind and was perhaps the last tenant. People pass through the city all the time. The British actress Kate Winslet is here today. Read more. Andheri is the Beverly Hills of North Bombay, that's how I explained it to Sarah because that's what it is. Actress Priyanka Chopra lives here. I mean not here but a short auto ride away. I mean c'mon, don't demean a man who has signed legal documents in almost thirty-one countries. I'm not a fool okay. There's a Mocha about ten minutes away and I can see Mainland China from the next building's window. So don't tell me just because you recognize your sweeper or your maid's names on the letterboxes that this must be a slum. People often buy flats under pseudonyms. There are rumours that Dawood Ibrahim is the owner of Wankhade Stadium which was his slum. No one calls that a slum now. No one says, 'Oh Sachin scored a century in the redeveloped pile of garbage.' No, they look at the grass and the floodlights and say, this place is for the who's who's who. Same with Prajakat. I'm the 'who' here.

Now a valid question to ask would be, 'Oh Arun, you're a CEO, what are you doing in a one-bedroom in Prajakat Housing Society, Andheri Kurla, that too in a store room for Blue Dart packages? Larry Elison of Sun Microsystems lives in a Japanese palace dismantled brick by brick and brought to San Francisco and you live on top of other people's letters?' To those people I say, you don't know what you don't know. When Ratan Tata was a baby, he was in a cot. Did he say, 'I am part of a billionaire industrialist's family, what am I doing with this much space?' He didn't. He made the best of it and then grew up, got out of the cot and slowly started living in the whole flat. In Colaba. This is like that. A starting point. When my new business venture becomes huge, I will get a door bell.

The thing is that I had all that in the past. Two to three bedrooms. Honestly, you don't need it. You sleep on one bed, not on three. Such waste. And in business, what you waste is what you lose. When I lost my wife, I decided to lose the bedrooms. When you are losing, lose all and start fresh. That's what I say. Ask any Sindhi person.

If Sarah ever reads this, she might say that when she entered my home/office, I was on my knees begging, but I will tell you right now, I was standing. I can look at her and say it to her face. No problem with that.

And the thing about cutting the electricity in my flat, that happened later. This is not that meeting. Point is, and I said this to Reliance Energy, I did not steal Mr Bhatti's meter box. I don't need to steal electricity. Why should I when I am a CEO.

Again, like the bedroom, the furniture too was gone. Antara had taken some of the furniture, and the children, because it was important where she was going. Anyway, furniture just suggests to me people who sit around all day. I don't sit, I move. On the move. Like Alexander. You know who sits? Old people. And they watch TV. First thing you do with furniture is sit down on it and then the TV and obviously, cricket. That's why I don't have either. And fuck cricket. When I build an empire, do you think people will stop and ask me the score?

Sarah had fifteen minutes and we had no place to sit. I knew I had to act quickly.

I took all my clothes and organized them in the shape of a carpet and lounged on them. Bhola got me a cigarette. I placed another one away from me near her. Basically, a hookah bar feel, minus the hookah and the cushions. She was definitely fooled.

I knew she was when she asked, 'What the hell are you doing?'

Point is, sometimes you have to create out of scarce resources. There's the American TV show *Apprentice*, where they were given dwarves to deliver pizzas all around Washington DC. This was far cleverer.

I was about to launch into my PowerPoint presentation, basically showing her the revenue potential of my new India but she began with a completely different thing. Venture capitalists do that to confuse you. When Bill Gates bought Hotmail, he didn't look at Hotmail's Sabeer Bhatia in the eye. I read that.

'Your fly is open.'

'Sorry?'

She was totally wrong. My fly was not open. I was wearing a suit but not the whole thing. My pants were my night suit pants. They don't have a zipper. Just buttons. It's called 'business casual'. It's very popular among IT entrepreneurs. If an IT professional was reading this, he would know exactly what I was talking about.

'Sarah, hit me.'

'What?'

'C'mon. Hit me.'

'You want me to hit you?'

'Yes.'

'Why?'

'You'll see what I'm made of. Iron. From head to toe. I have a term for me, "Man of Steel".'

One of the early lessons I learnt in the business world was that if you are weak, come across as strong. Physically. It's called posturing. That's why Ratan Tata works out.

'Sarah, I need cash.'

'There's a fucking recession. Mercedez is going bankrupt, and *you* want cash?'

'Yes. No not there, don't hit me there, that's my liver. Here, here. Yes. What do you think huh? Solid. Nothing breaks me because I don't break. I don't cry. Slowly, little slowly. Am I something or what?'

'You're an idiot.'

'I am begging.'

'You're not begging.'

'I can beg.'

'Don't beg.'

You have to move between having the upper hand and having no hand at all. It's like chess. If chess was a hundred-metre race. As someone wise once said, 'It's all a game'.

'Are you wearing your night suit?'

'*Yes. But* it's Armani. Heathrow duty free. I shop only at the best places.'

'People worldwide are shutting businesses. I don't know what I was thinking when I funded your call centre. You've spent my fund's investment on a failed business. People in New York laugh at me when I mention you. Now you're saying, not only are you not sorry but that you want more money from me?'

One thing I've learnt about women over the years is that they exaggerate. That's just how it is. Especially women who are in a hurry to catch a flight. You have to tackle the situation with a compliment.

'You speak better than Obama. Gimme five.'

'This posturing you're doing. What would you call this?'

'Vision. I call it vision.'

'I call it suicide.'

She had hit the bull's eye. I was coming to suicide from a different angle but she didn't take an angle, she came to it straight. Doesn't matter how minds meet between business partners, the main thing is, they do. I heard Hewlett and Packard met in a toilet.

'Ha ha...you're kidding right? Funny...'

'No.'

'That *is* my new business plan. Suicide.'

That's the thing with negotiation. Whatever the topic is, bring it back to you.

'You're going to need a good lawyer.'

'Look, if I told you ten years ago that all major American credit card calls would be outsourced to India, you'd say what?'

'Stop smoking crack.'

'But you invested in 1800 Repair and you may have lost money, but undeniably, other companies are getting home appliances repaired in India. So the thing has happened. Just not with my company. So who is smoking crack now? You say?'

'I am.'

'That's right, negro.'

What I am very good at is contemporary American phrases. I can use the phrase they used and turn it and use it against the user. It's called turn of the phrase. There's another one—what's up dog. It's a youngster phrase but people use it to talk to other people. The fools don't realize that 'what's up dog' is meant to be applied when talking to a dog. I've spent a lot of time over there and picked up these things. Observations. Same thing with 'negro'.

'You're misusing the phrase,' said Sarah.

'Since 2001, the American customer service industry has relocated to India almost entirely. The outsourcing business is now valued over twenty billion. So whether its New York Life Insurance, Verizon cell phones, Pfizer prescriptions, MasterCard, iTunes help, Banana Republic sweater returns, Ford GPS System—we do it all.'

In a sales pitch, having facts and figures is key.

'Everyone knows labour is cheap in India. Okay, so you've read Thomas Friedman,' said Sarah, nonchalantly.

'I don't read books one can buy at Mahim traffic signals. In fact, I don't read. There are some forty million Indians who are employable, English-speaking college graduates. People I can hire. For my new, new thing.'

Wherever possible, use live examples for dramatic effect to illustrate your numbers. I had Bhola to illustrate mine.

'Sir, chai,' said Bhola as he brought in the tray.

'Like this guy. My cook, Bhola. Eh Bhola, say something in English to madam.'

'Hello, sir.'

'English...English.'

'Malum nahin, sir.'

'Ja yaha se. Phat...idiot.'

Sometimes your example will fail you. You have to refocus. 'Anyway, so forty million English-speaking Indians and I don't have a single one in my company. In fact, I don't even have a company. Why? Why am I not tapping the ass of India?'

That's called street talk. When you throw in phrases of the man on the US street. 'Tap that ass' is used by rappers. I added India to improvise.

'Ermm, I don't quite understand what you mean but if you're asking why you don't have a company, it's mainly because of your bad decisions. And if you're asking why forty million young Indians don't work in outsourcing, I would say that they could actually be doing something meaningful with their lives.'

'Chillax, that's my word. This is India, *deude*. Meaningful means money. Meaningful doesn't mean becoming some homo artist and fooling around in the Himalayas. Yoga and all that nonsense came from you guys.'

'Yoga is from your Hindu scripture. Yog is concentration.'

'Look, *my* Hindu books say whateverr the whateverr. Most people here live in garbage and are trying to get out of it. The slumdog world is not flat. It is a ladder with the dog barking at the bottom. So I ask you again—why don't I have forty million employees? C'mon tell me, tell me.'

Create tension and put the other person on the back foot. If it's a woman, as in my case, the back heel.

'Well, in pure business terms, Americans aren't outsourcing enough.'

'Clever. That's why you have nice boobs and I went to Shriram College of Commerce, which brings me to...'

When you reach the climax, always have a PowerPoint slide.

'...suicide. Various research reports on the American Public Health industry predict that one out of every three Americans is currently suicidal. That's a customer base of a hundred million people. Today, when you want to die, you call a 1-800 number and someone in the US answers. Why? Why pay so much to US people?'

'They are all trained psychiatric professionals. Masters in trauma therapy.'

'Fuck all that, man. Woman. We will train. You think only Americans know how to die? Read *The Times of India*; people commit suicide here twice a day, and over every small thing. Exam failure, girlfriend, loan repayment...we are fucking gurus in trauma. This is Bombay man, the Disneyland of trauma. But I will have state-of-the-art training. So my employees will be Indian only in body and appearance. But American in spirit, aspiration and dying.'

You always know in a good sales pitch when you are winning. The other person pauses. Always follow up market research with a speech where it looks like you will almost cry. I was not crying because I am a man's man but every man is different.

'What is the market potential?'

The fish had bitten the bait. I don't normally use a fishing example in business but in this case, that's what was happening. I had thrown the fishing rod and she was swimming away. My speech was the bait. She got hungry. I caught her. 'Now you're talking like a hot chick. Our numbers only capture registered manic-depressed Americans—not those with the potential for depression. And with the recession, environmental destruction going as planned, oil shortage, food shortage, inflation, we can only expect the depression numbers to rise.'

'What are you showing me? It just says 17, 35, 46, 87, 197.'

'They are numbers. And they are rising.' That brings me to my next point. It doesn't matter if you have the right numbers to back up your business idea but always have numbers.

'This is completely crazy.'

'If this becomes the next Google, if this is indeed the next ten-billion market, do you want to say you missed the boat? Do you?'

Always position an opportunity to an investor, not by what they might get but what they might miss out on. Nobody wants to miss out on a party. Even if there is no party.

'How much do you want?'

The first lesson when throwing out a number is not to throw out any number. Think of the number you want and increase it by one. And the second lesson is whatever number they throw back, say no. What happened that day with Sarah was a proper negotiation. She gave a little, I gave a little. In the end, we both won.

'Four hundred million dollars.'

'I'll give you eighteen thousand.'

'Done.'

Employees (machines of the twenty-first century)

Ten days later, we moved into our offices at the Prestige Business Centre in a pretty important part of Mumbai. Later, I told my secretary, Bhola—yes Bhola my cook—I promoted him, sent him to Anuradha Bhasin's SPEAKEZYEE English classes, and he's my PA now. He knows Microsoft, new India, social mobility…if you don't know what that means, you should read Chetan Bhagat and learn. Anyway, I told Bhola, 'Look, it doesn't matter that we are four hours from Nariman Point. The point is that we are facing the west, towards the US, where our market is waiting to die.' Bhola looked a bit confused but I told him that he'd soon understand.

Most call centres make the fatal mistake of hiring a lot of people at their inception. Look at Tata and ITC. Filled with thousands of 20 year old bastards right from day one without the customer base. I'm not into that. Very soon, you're burning cash, and I don't want to go back to Sarah, in my house, wearing my Armani night suit and say, deude, I burnt cash because my office is filled with young people drinking coffee and not enough Americans dying. I want to spend cash and get more cash. It's a unique business strategy I know, but that's who I am—unique. So I thought I would start as a specialist call centre.

I was debating between hiring either twenty-five people or just two people, and I decided on two. It's like ordering at Mughal Durbar where you can always ask for more roomali roti. My first two employees would be the first two roomali rotis and then I'd get the others hot, instead of them just sitting cold. No, not in a…not sexual… Look, I know what happens to people who are into that okay. Alimony. Soon, they catch you with too much cologne in a four-star B town with thongs and a teenager from Uzbekistan. Or your wife finds some sms about some declined Amex payment to Miss Divine in Bangkok and you get truly fucked. I can't be into that. I have equity investors.

So I put in a post on Monster.com. The fuckers charged me four thousand bucks for it. Bastards. I'm giving them business, and they're charging me money for it? Their customer representative, Parvati, tried to explain to me that that's their business model—commission based—but who do they think I am? Some old fucker who only uses Gmail?

But finally it was up. The ad headline read, 'Start-up Looking for Self-Starters in Mumbai.'

Clever, right, to use 'start-up' and 'self-starter' in one sentence? I want people to think that this is a fun place to work. Like Google. They can immediately see that the boss is a funny guy. He puns. And I wanted people to get that. If you don't get subtlety, you won't understand the US. Period.

They say our greatest asset is our hundreds of millions of young, educated middle-class. Then why did I get only twelve applications? Anyways, fuck that. I don't care. I said, when we are bigger than General Electric, I will have twelve people just doing my human resource management. When you're hiring, always look for how people respond to your ad. That way you immediately get to know who they are. No one will give you this insight. But take it from me.

I picked two to interview because I needed two. That's a limited choice, you may say. In fact, that's no choice. If you interview two, you have to hire two. But see, here's the thing. I screened. I am a screener. Look like a hawk and then hunt like a deer, that's my hiring tactic.

The first two emailed responses said, 'Fuck you.' Now while that might show initiative, drive and leadership, it already shows me that they have no respect for the company email. How would a lady in Utah feel if she got a 'fuck you' email just before putting her head in an oven? Not nice. So they were immediately fired. Then this female applicant wrote one little sentence, 'Are you Sudha?' This told me two things about the person. One, that she prefers to work for a woman. Two, that she's using company time to chat with her friend Sudha. Disqualified.

The rest of the responses I couldn't understand because they were in Telugu and said something about voting for Chiranjeevi.

Then I got to the last two. They really knew what they were doing.

Ramesh18999537@gmail.com said, 'Sir, I'd like an interview,' and KoolKattRashmi@bsnl.co.in said, 'Yes.'

I like her better. Precise and not wasting the boss's time, even though I didn't know what she was saying yes to. It didn't matter. She had my attention with her briefness.

I called them in together early in the morning. 11 am. Always do that to candidates. It makes them nervous. And make sure they know they are both waiting for the same thing. You can tell them they will both be hired, no problem, but make sure they see each other. That's the thing to make them nervous. They do it in Iraq. It's called disorientation but the technical term is Russian Roulette.

Ramesh looked a little like a younger version of the great Hollywood actor Gulshan Grover but with a thin moustache. I immediately took a liking to him because I like Mr Grover's body of work. Especially in the movie where he was the molester of an Olympic swimmer, played by the very talented actress, Pamela Anderson. In business, this is free association. That's why when you think of Mumbai developers, you think thieves. Same.

I decided to fuck with Ramesh's body first. Mostly his tongue. By which, I naturally mean his accent. Swami Vivekananda said if you mess with the body, the mind will follow. I changed the situation a little. In my case, Rashmi would follow.

'Howdy. I'm Arun Gupta, CEO, 1888 Dial India. Who are you bro?'

'My name is Ramesh.'

'Fuck no.'

'Sorry, sorry, sir, my name is Greg.'

'And where do you live, Greg?'

'In Mumbai like you, I...'

'No bastard...' I threw a stress ball at him that the guy from Airtel Broadband had given me when he set up the networks. What I was really doing was playing good cop/bad cop. Thing is though, I was both cops.

'Sir, sorry, sir, I mean I was born in Texas *and* went to university there.'

'Where?'

'University of...Texas.'

'And what do you do for a living, Greg?'

'I am a certified healthcare professional trained by the state of Maharashtra.'

'Phat.'

One word here. Intimidation.

'Sorry, Pennsylvania, sir.'

'Nice.'

'And what makes you happy?'

'Saving American lives. I like to protect my fellow citizens, sir.'

'Do you know what this means? Aaj se tum kya ho?' Never stop with the questions. Layer questions on top of questions without allowing the candidate to answer them. It's like making a question cake that you can't eat. My philosophy is that if you can't eat it, no one should be able to.

'Aaj se mein Suicide Watch ka employee hoon, sir.'

'Chut.'

'Sorry, sir, sorry, aj se mein American hoon.'

'In *English* fucker!'

'From today, I am American.'

'And remember the company motto?'

'This is not a call centre. This is a hospital with phone lines instead of beds.'

That was a trick question, as the Americans would say. We officially have no company motto. That's just a line I wrote and put on the door under the name of the company on an A4 paper. I was going to get a plaque—some call it an insignia—but the bloody thing costs eight thousand rupees. I had to choose between a plaque and phone lines and I went with the phone lines because you need those in a call centre. And already with the shared bathroom fees at the business centre, really high, electricity, stationary, I'm already fucked. But the important thing is that Ramesh read it. Even though I wrote it with a marker and cut it and wrote over it.

'Excellent. And do you have what it takes to be an American person? What do you have? Tell me... tell me.'

I keep a baseball bat in my office. Most other CEOs keep photos with prime ministers. I don't. I was hitting Ramesh a little, shouting a little, I'll admit. Whatever. It's for character building. They do it in Guantanamo Bay and look at the results.

'Yes, sir. I have watched *Rambo*. Means, I can do anything.'

That was a good answer. A go-getter. Someone who goes and gets. I like that.

'Welcome to the 1888 Dial India team.'

Now, before I interviewed Rashmi, I was pissed off with Ramesh. He took the keys to the bathroom and took almost seven and a half minutes in there. The people from the next cabin, Cairn Energy, could not go. And they had paid for unlimited toilet access. So the business centre said they would charge me extra for five and a half minutes (2 minutes was the free toilet time I had negotiated). I am usually a cool person, both in terms of looks and all that, and also in terms of calm. Yes, you guessed it—I know both meanings of cool. It comes from experience. But this time, I lost it with the second meaning.

What I am trying to say is that I lost it. First, I shouted at him but shouting is never enough. Mamata Banerjee shouts, the people of *Times Now* shout, but what happens? We go to sleep and wake up the next day totally forgetting about them. So

I had to do something more powerful. I took his shoe and I told him that he couldn't leave till he figured out some way of making it up to me. In business schools they give you case studies; this was somewhat similar.

Also, I understand the importance of drama. I am a keen observer of the movies of Mr Sanjay Leela Bhansali. He has a beard and uses the dramatic in drama. I am clean-shaven and use the dramatic in business situations. Same tool, two results. Wharton calls this double-value creation.

So when Rashmi walked in, I had just finished shouting at Ramesh. I was sitting at my desk, with a shoe in my hand. I told Ramesh to wait in the file cabinet. It must have confused her. Good. She was hoping to say hello but I got up and walked into the file cabinet. One word—improvisation. That's what I was doing. And I said some gibberish to Ramesh loudly in the cabinet. Now they were both totally confused. Excellent. Two stones, two birds. You know what I mean.

But seriously though, that is the only way to keep employees on their toes. If they don't know what's coming next, or what came before or ideally, what's happening in the present, you'll get their attention. One is always prepared. That's how you prepare the next generation. The Japanese auto makers can learn something from me.

I should mention that sometimes on my computer I click on iTunes and play music. And this was one of those times. That's the latest way.

Another distraction for interviewee—audio. You can see how I was combining visual distraction (shoe, closet) and audio distraction (iTunes) to create a holistic distraction. That's the only way to test an interviewee holistically.

In the army, they would wake you up at 4 am for a fake terrorist attack drill and there would be fake shootings and bombs are heard. Here, I was going around with a shoe and music was heard. Same tactic.

I came out of the closet, went to my desk and shut down iTunes, How do I have the latest songs? One US credit card. (Don't be impressed. I used to have five). Then I focused on the woman.

'So, Rashmi, you're married?'

'No.'

'Virgin?'

'Um. Yes.'

'Fuckin' hell, wow. Young. Y-O-N-G. It's okay with me. Conservative. Conser…vative. Family. In Hispanic, *familia*.'

I know quite a bit of Spanish. Today, business is global, and you have to speak many languages. If you don't know what I mean, watch the HSBC ads.

'Arranged?'

'Sorry?'

'Will you be sold in an arranged marriage?'

'I will try to avoid arranged marriage, sir, but my mother is strict. My father is dead, and that was his dying wish.'

'Small town caste bullshit. Whateverrr. I got no issues. BUT in your twenties, you should be out on the street in a micro-mini, striking guys out.' I did a bowling gesture.

'Sir, I have gone bowling. I understand you.'

'So you know how to play the game, flirtittilation, you know...you know?'

I was obviously trying to connect bowling with flirting. Striking guys out meant guys would pass out seeing her looks. Honestly, no one would pass out seeing her but I was giving her a compliment. But she didn't get it. Humour is such a niche thing.

'In Andheri, there is Pleasure Lanes Bowling, sir. My last call centre had an offsite there with Bacardi sponsorship. I went.'

'That's good. You know what my term for that is? Open-minded. Open is better than closed-minded. An open family is non-veg. A closed family is a... is fucked up. All religious. What are your hobbies, chiquita? Wait, I'll go first. I am Arun, I don't want to drum to my own beat but I guess you could call me the boss. Because I am. My favourite movie of all time is *Top Gun*. Cruise controool, baby. I'm a beast at table tennis. Growl. In the US, it's known as Ping Pong.'

'I love *Indian Idol*, sir, on Star Plus.'

'Fuck Star TV. No no, lady...you'll need total westernification. See, Americans are individuals—that's the main thing. What's your main thing? That's the thing, you need your own thing. The thing that sets you apart from the rest, makes you cool. Do you cook at home?'

'Yes, sir. My mother makes...'

'Stop. Cooking is done in jails only. Americans only eat Cup o' Noodles. It's like Maggi but white. For white people. What music do you like?'

'Sonu Nigam.'

She started singing some rubbish. Honestly, really bad.

'Sonu Noganna work...noganna work.' That was a good pun.

'But, sir, you were listening to same song.'

'Sshh. My computer's defective. Listen, have you heard of a rapper called the Menimem?'

'Huh?'

'Neminems...I am the slim shaded...'

'Sir, Eminem?'

'Eminememem...listen to it. It will be important. You must know these things. He's the dog's balls, negro.'

'Sir, I don't know that sport *but* I am very keen on involving myself into all American things. I am very eager, sir. That's my nature.'

'I'm not convinced. Seduce me. Why convince?'

'Sir?'

'I mean convince me. Why suicide?' Look, if you work the hours I do, sometimes you're allowed to confuse your sentences. Work, jetlag...ask any pilot. Nobody's perfect, even though I am almost there.

'As you are probably into noticing...,' She kept talking but I got up and checked on Ramesh in the file cabinet to see if he was still alive. He was. I had forgotten about him. '…I am having the American accent, so no training I'll need. That's what I am, a call centre person already. Ready to jump into it. In my current job, I am receiving underwear orders from Hanes His Way, and I'm bored. Now I want to do suicide.'

'You are 100 percent sure?'

'100 percent suicide.'

Underwear to suicide was not a big jump. Richard Branson moved from music to airlines. But it was a move nonetheless. 'Chicmangalore, I like you, and when I like someone I don't care where they are, like in jail or hiding from income tax. I don't care if people say, "Don't mix with him, he's a criminal." All I can say to them is "fuck you". Fuck all of you who have no guts because I have a gut instinct about people. And my guts say that you need my pole.'

'Sorry, sir?'

I pressed my bell. It's under my table. My dad had it in his office at Mantralaya. And he pressed it, when, you know, he was accepting something under the table and he didn't want the peon to come. Now I use it when I want the peon to come. See how India has changed. Business is transparent nowadays. It means God is trying to tell India something. 'Bhola, pole lao…pole leke ao…accha se…dekh ke…thik se dekho…fan hain…fuck up mat karo…'

Bhola brought in the pole and put it down. It was my favourite thing. I turned to Rashmi and asked, 'Huh…what do you think?'

'Sir, it's a pole...'

'Yeah, yeah but a pole for what...?'

'Pole...I don't know.'

'Pole dancing. See, I think a membership at Gold's Gym or whatever those other rubbish call centres are offering is a waste of time if you have your own pole. Sexy dancing is the world's best fitness programme. Forget diets. I know what you're thinking, that it's like sexual striptease. Like the Bangkok chicks but that's where the world is mistaken. That's where the Customs guys were mistaken. That's why I told them, "Yeh sex ka item nahi hain. Yeh exercise ka item hain. Isko sex ke list mein mut dalo. Isko sex wali list mein kaise dal sakhte hain? Yeh exercise ki list mein ana chaihiye." See, there are two kinds of pole dancing.' I pulled out a DVD for her. 'This one is *Carmen Electra's Collection of Horny Music* for exercising. And then there's another one called *Carmen Electra's Dirty Lap-Dance*. That's the dirty one. This one is for housewives and college graduates.'

'Sir, did I get the job?'

'Yes. Why do you think you get the pole? Some places have a signing bonus. I give this to the deserving. They give five stars to US Generals. That's small and made of metal. This is big and made of metal. Better "think out of the box...that has money", that's my recruiting philosophy.'

Sometimes people aren't quick enough to be on my wavelength. I had hired her fifteen minutes ago.

Home life

A few days after hiring my staff, I realized I would have to deal with an ugly truth. Two words that are much worse in business than Tax Default—Personal Life. These are accounts of what happened in my newly recruited employees' personal lives soon after the interviews.

There is a very simple rule I have about personal life. It's unnecessary, especially when you are young. Michelangelo spent his teenage years sleeping in a basement and working like a dog in his patron's studio. He never wanted the night off because some new DJ was in town or some girl was sitting alone at Café Coffee Day. He became a genius by working twenty-four hours a day, not sleeping for ten or twelve years. That's what it takes to be a genius.

Another example. Lots of people say Sachin Tendulkar started playing cricket when he was 15. They were wrong. He started when he was eight months old. Before he could walk. That's what genius is. Look at Mark Andreessen, the guy who created the Internet or the guy who invented Gelato. They never took time off to go for some holiday to Goa and drink and urinate all over the place. Read about Osama Bin Laden. He began terrorizing people from when he was a very young boy. He didn't say, 'Oh, let me take an hour off and go and see a Farhan Akhtar movie'. That's dedication.

The thing is, whoever you are in your professional life, that's who you are in your personal life because you are a person. Lots of people forget that. That's key in business—being a person. Therefore the personal life is what you bring to work every day. So whatever you are doing after work is the same thing. Inseparable. The person is common here.

Rashmi and Ramesh received their offer letters.

It wasn't really a formal offer letter, just something I got Bhola to type. There were some small errors, like Ramesh's name (Roshmesh) and the name of the company (1-888-Dial-Indy). I tried to explain to both that there was no hurry to tell anyone—more people, family, parents—whatever, because it would only lead to more questions. They didn't listen. Some rubbish reason that they they lived with them and couldn't lie to them—some old school nonsense like that.

The thing is, I didn't tell Ramesh and Rashmi just how many details I wanted to know about their home conversations. It's good that they understood that I meant a lot. Actually, all of it. Honestly though, back then if you asked me if I'd put people's private family conversations in a book, I'd have said maybe. Only because Facebook was still new so there were still some people who believed in privacy or whateverrr. That's all gone now, thankfully.

Rashmi has a mother. There will be more on her later. After an interview, some people ask their employees to come back the next day. I didn't. I put her to work immediately. But it wasn't a tough shift. Three people—two in Nebraska with bullet wounds, and one fellow in San Francisco who was stabbed. And she was out early at 3 am. Still, like Gandhi cared about the nation, I care about my employees. Yes, there was a concern that she's a girl and she might get raped and all that, but more importantly, she had my pole. Don't forget that during that interview, Ramesh was in the filing cabinet. I asked Ramesh to get out and escort her home.

He had gone to sleep in there. I liked his dedication. Others would have complained or cried or run back home or whatever. He quietly went to sleep without disturbing me. I realized this quality would one day help him. And me. In a non-closet scenario. That's another thing about qualities. Once you have them, you can drop them in situations. Like closet quality, in a kidnapping situation. Silent sleeping equals kidnappers might let you live.

That's how the CEO of HP can become the CEO of Sun Microsystems. Different situation. You don't need to know how to photocopy. You need qualities.

Rashmi and her mother live in a small flat because they live off their father's pension. The mother apparently sleeps in the living room so poor

Rashmi can't even sneak in totally smashed with three men.

That's a big problem in modern India with women. Where do you fuck? Real estate issues. All these builders like Unitech and DLF may solve the beauty problem—the new towers are nice looking but they are not solving the fucking problem. Builders are only catering to five bedrooms with pools for Sindhi suit makers in Hong Kong. But see, I am also a big supporter of women's rights so it worries me. I know Antara didn't know this side of me when she left and she'll say I don't listen or whatever, but I do. Not just to her, but to the problems of all women.

My employees tip-toed quietly into the flat. It was early morning or very late night. If you are good in our line of work, you shouldn't be able to tell. I had told Ramesh to drop her to her doorstep but I think he took initiative and stepped in. I don't blame him. He was carrying her pole for her and its heavy. I am a considerate man. I know how difficult it might be for a young woman to carry a large aluminum pole into an auto rikshaw. That's my feminism side again.

'Shhh, Mr Ramesh, my mother doesn't know anything about call centres. She thinks I'm a real doctor in the emergency room at Lilavati. I have a friend there who re-routes my landline calls to my cell. That's how I manage to work all night for so long.'

'Okay. This pole is really heavy. Can I put it down somewhere?'

'Sure,' said Rashmi.

Ramesh put the pole down with a clatter and it immediately woke Rashmi's mother. That's the problem with slums. Noise spreads. 'You're late. Was Amitabh admitted again?'

'No, mama, just some Americans.'

'Accident? Terrorist attack?'

'No, see, the hospital is so happy with my work that they have promoted me to being a doctor on the phone. I now help Americans with emergencies. We have opened a new wing called the Lilavati Phone Wing.'

'Why do you need to save lives? English no? Life is life. And who is this boy?'

'Ramesh…he's a nurse.'

'Hello aunty. I'm Nurse Ramesh.'

Improvising—good. If ever a man is found in your bed naked and you are a young woman, also naked, you need to improvise. With words. She was learning early. Same logic applies if Income Tax shows up.

'What is this?' She was looking at my pole now.

The mother was quite snoopy. I knew a Customs guy like her, Khondke. Wonder if they are related.

'A pole. My new boss gave me a pole.'

Rashmi. Straight answer.

'Why did he give you a pole?'

Go to sleep old lady, that's what I would have said.

'For pole dancing. It's a gift.'

Exactly. She could also have said bonus but never mind. High-pressure situations, you improvise. Rashmi was thinking on her feet. Like Gautam Gambhir.

'What is the point of dancing around a pole?'

This is why I prefer America. After a certain age, all parents are put in an old age home. Specifically to avoid questions like this.

'It's like jogging. I do it also.' Ramesh came to her rescue.

That's why two is better than one. Doubles the effort straight away.

'Show me.'

This mother would not stop.

'Huh?' Ramesh was taken aback with the mother's forthrightness. Understandably. Imagine if someone asked me, 'Why do you have a Swiss bank account?' I mean, is there no privacy anymore?

'Ma, he's just a nurse.'

That's what I call back-referencing. Rashmi mentioned he was a nurse when she introduced him to crazy old mom. Now she connected that to her present lie. Some call this two lies. I call it genius.

'A dancing nurse. He said.'

Rashmi's mother must have had some professional training. Only the CBI can interrogate like this. I know because…never mind.

'Aunty, I…'

Like for Like. I like Rashmi more. Ramesh had no answer here. Idiot.

'Ma, he has to go. He has dying patients.'

See what she did here. Going into a nurse's daily schedule. This is improvising at its best. Better than acting. Tom Cruise needs a script. Not Rashmi. And it was almost 4 am. Tom Cruise would have been in bed by now.

'Two minutes. C'mon show me.'

Relentless Aunty. That's what she is. Not just aunty. Even the IT department gives up after four raids but not this one.

'Aunty, I'll need some music.'

Finally, a Ramesh comeback. Decoy. Throw her off track. Some companies start shell companies to stash black money in Mauritius. Ramesh says he cannot strip because there is no music. Same thing. Different tools.

'Music...what is that DVD you're holding?'

The mother's definitely had some IAS training apart from interrogation. It's not easy to be this annoying.

'Nothing,' said Rashmi.

Good Rashmi. Under interrogation, always Deny everything. That's the first lesson in business. Actually, that's the second. The first is shred all legal contracts and emails.

'Hand it over...*Carmen Electra's Collection of Horny Music*?'

Again old people doing what they do best. Value Judgment. Dismissing Horny Music without listening. Imagine if people had thrown out Microsoft Windows just because at the time, all other programs were MS DOS. Where would we be if we all became sarcastic like Relentless Aunty and not give things a chance? I'd be writing this book on papyrus. And you don't even get that in Andheri.

'It's for health reasons, aunty.' Two more points to Ramesh for showing some more thinking on the feet. Will be helpful during any sort of government raid.

Ramesh told me the next day that he had to dance to the song 'Don't Funk with My Heart' by *The Black Eyed Peas* (I'm not racist, that is the name) till Rashmi switched off the DVD. Rashmi told me that he was quite qualified in striptease, based on what she had seen of experts on Star World. That's a valuable business talent—skill sets in areas outside your core expertise.

'That's a brief summary, aunty.'

'Exactly what kind of hospital gives this kind of nurse training?'

'Our boss, Arun, says that nurses need to be fit.'

Ramesh was right. But not only that, dancing improves your heart rate too.

'For which patients do you do this dance?'

'Our boss is a nice man, mama, he also gave Ramesh and me two special passes to a new Water Theme Park in Bhandup. Naren Enterprises Dirty Splash Water World. Gala Opening with fireworks on Saturday, live on SAB TV. Can I go?'

I forgot to mention that I get these free passes every year from the place I order Chicken Makhni.

I always gave it to Bhola first but he doesn't have swimming trunks.

Right before Rashmi was leaving I threw it in as an added bonus to the pole signing bonus. A top-up. In American sales terms, it's called incentives. Incentives are not bonus because it's spelt differently. It means the thing sprinkled on top of a bonus. Like a topping on the topping. The Crème De La Crème De la Crème.

'No.'

This mother was worse than other mothers. Usually, in my previous ventures, parents used to say 'You are awful' or 'My child wasted two years with you'. No one turned down an incentive.

'Fake ocean waves coordinated with *Slumdog* soundtrack, aunty.'

Ramesh got into the specifics which is always better than high level. Actually, not always better. In Suresh Kalmadi's Commonwealth Games case, it did not work.

'No.'

This was not a mother. It was a "no" machine.

'They have bumper cars endorsed by Adnan Sami, ma.'

Honestly, I hadn't read the free pass. Had I known Adnan Sami or whateverrr, I might have gone myself. He's Canadian.

'No.'

You can't help but wonder if the mother has broken down. Like a bad toy. And all she could say was no.

'There's a "Wear a bikini, get a free bikini" contest aunty'.

Now Ramesh was lying. Which is fine. But this was the wrong audience. In some audiences, a bikini will entice. Not when it is in reference to someone's girl child. Then you want to avoid nudity. I'm not going to get into how I know this but I learnt the hard way.

'What?'

Finally, the mother broke her no spell. It was almost as bad as the Japanese economy going through nine quarters of negative growth.

'Our boss Arun says that India has changed. It's a sexy place now. Everyone should wear a bikini.'

Clever girl. I told her that during the coffee break. After that Nebraska guy shot himself.

'Beta, I don't understand what all this means.'

She should have admitted this right from the beginning. Would have saved us all this trouble. What she doesn't understand is where India is going. Away from her, that's what.

'If I can't go on Saturday, I want to go to the Khar KFC now. I am a Gold member. I am eligible for a KFC Golden Shower.'

Other KFC Gold Members are noted later in the book but Rashmi should be proud of her achievement. It's an elite list that you can get on only after a substantial consumption of fried chicken.

'I made parathas and stayed up all night to feed you.'

Another thing about Indian parents I don't get, this whole cooking mind games thing. Kid steps out of the house and they furiously start fucking around in the kitchen as if doing the world a big-ass favour no one asked for. Hello lady, no one asked you to do it but you did it anyway and now it's your cool young Indian's fault that she won't eat? It's a trap. Never fall for it. It's almost like the Russian Cold War. Paratha is the Bay of Pigs. Rashmi is Cuba. Relentless Aunty is Russia. Never go into the Bay of Pigs of Paratha. I know what you're thinking. You didn't ask for the Paratha Bay of Pigs. She would do it regardless. If it isn't paratha, then it'll be something else, like sabzi. Same result. You can change the dish but the result is still the Bay of Pigs crisis. In that case, who will blink first? Kennedy did not blink.

'Throw it.'

And nor did Rashmi. I was proud of her.

'Then I'm going to throw away this pole.'

Ooh nice. Mother elevates cold war to hot war.

'No you're not. It's mine.'

There was pushing and pulling over the pole. Which I liked. Something I introduced into this house was already causing a change. That's the thing about a new idea—whatever shape it takes, in this case a pole—it will change you. And fighting for a new idea always shows who is in power. Sometimes in soap opera serials, there is background music to highlight a moment like this. It's sad that we do not have that in life.

Ramesh used this moment to run.

I think these serials aren't helping to make these mothers quieter like everyone thinks. My opinion is, it's making them louder. They feel they can stand up to their children and take away their poles. About five years ago, parents would never have had this sort of audacity. Point is, in every household there's a mother and/or a father who always has problems when employees join me. In this case it's both. No probs. I'll deal with it. Anyways, I will say to them what they said of Russy Modi's tenure at TISCO: 'His time was up'.

I am not one to interfere in my employees' private life but I like to be informed. Not of all the details, but maybe 99 percent of them. I know for a fact that Ramesh has a father who is a bastard. I didn't know it then but later...anyway. He also has a sister who often dresses like women on Zoom TV but she wouldn't be on TV. Not hot enough. She's a college girl who looks like a college girl, not a college girl in TV serials or Karan Johar films. She's a real college girl. Yes, scary. Again, I shouldn't talk about people outside work. That book on the guy who invented Penicillin didn't. Actually, it did. It talked about wanting to work extremely hard to find a drug to cure a life-threatening disease to save his child and build a billion-dollar company as a result. This is like that. Not gossip.

So in Ramesh's home situation, about this father thing, I had a term for him. My term for him is in the next paragraph. Wait for it.

The next morning, Ramesh's father was home, reading his newspaper or whatever. That's what backward people do—people who don't get news on their BlackBerry. People without Wi-fi. People behind the times. That's why I have a term for them. Old. And he gave Old my letter.

That's the other benefit of working in outsourcing that a lot of Indians miss. Breakfast with the family. Except, instead of going out after it for a long day of work, the employee goes to sleep after a long night of work. So he/she sees breakfast as dinner and enjoys it more. Same benefit, different exit. Remember the famous quote from some British writer fucker, every exit is an entrance somewhere else? To me, I change it to say, in the home of every outsourcing employee, every dinner is a breakfast somewhere else.

'Suicide? People kill themselves and you save them on the phone?' was Old's question to Ramesh.

'Yes, papa.'

'Like catching practice in cricket, papa.' That was Anjali—Ramesh's sister. From the name you can guess what kind of society they belong to. Yes, middle class.

'Yes but instead of a ball, you catch a person,' said Ramesh.

'When Americans are dying, they don't know the call is outsourced?' asked Old.

'When we are on the phone we are Americans. Americans saving Americans. That's my boss' business plan, papa.'

'Why are you talking like that?'

'Like what?' asked Ramesh.

'Like there is a big piece of fish in your mouth.'

'That's how I normally speak. It's my accent, papa.'

'Why do you have an accent? We live in Vashi,' said Old, aghast at his son.

Another sign of middle classness. And you are beginning to see, I hope, why his father was a bastard. This father-son chat was just a way for the father to ask questions but really say, 'Oh, look, I'm the boss'. Like a twisted version of a Crorepati show where both Amitabh and your dad were the hosts asking you the money questions but then throwing in a 'What are you doing up so late taking part in this show?' just to mess with you. That's what Old does. Mind games. Not like my mind games which are straightforward. Old's mind games take U-turns.

'My boss, Arun, says without an American accent, you're a piece of shit.'

'I'm a piece of shit? I'm your father! I am an IAS officer!'

'No no, papa, he means in life. To be someone you have to have an accent.'

'But if Americans find out they are being saved from Powai, they will kill themselves even quicker. Tell your boss that.'

'That's why they must believe totally in my American persona, Greg.'

'Who?'

'Gregory from Pittsburg, USA. My boss says, if we believe in our American personality, the customers will believe it too.'

Exactly.

'My name is Gautam. I have been Under-Secretary of the Rural Development, Government of Maharashtra for twenty-two years. The Ministry of Rural Development has not asked me to change my name to Bhura because I work with farmers.'

I don't really have a problem with Old. I have a problem with where people like him are going. Backwards. Past. Always quoting history. Whereas me, I'm always looking forward. That's the difference between old India and me. Direction.

'My boss says in today's India, to be someone in life, you have to be someone else.'

'So the only way to do well at this job is lying? Like a con man?'

Old started to get really worked up.

Negative. So negative. Such a fine line between positive and negative.

'No no, papa. See if they die, we lose points. If we save them, we collect points and get a promotion. I'm not a con man, I'm a doctor...with points.'

'You will not do this job. This discussion is over.' Old put away his newspapers with a finality.

'I've signed the papers, Gautam.'

'Who is Gautam?' asked Old.

'In the US, people call their parents by their first names.'

Exactly. I would even go further and say Old Gautam.

'If we lived in the US, you can call me Santa Claus for all I care. Here, in my house, you will call me papa.'

Old missed the point.

'There was a signing bonus of rupees ten thousand. With the bonus, I went to McDonald's.' With that, Ramesh left the room.

That's the other thing I need to change about Ramesh. He likes Bollywood. Especially Bobby Deol. No idea who that is. I may have seen one or two or all of his movies but that's accidental. Around 3 am most nights, my remote control gets stuck on Star Gold. I will get it fixed.

'Where did Ramesh go?'

'He's showing you something, papa,' said Anjali.

'I'm back.'

'What is this, Ramesh?'

'A cut out of Bobby Deol.'

'What is he doing in my house?'

'I took part in the McDonald's Pagal Dhamaka Touch a Star Contest. I won. Next Tuesday, we can touch Bobby Deol at the Vashi InOrbit.'

'Ooh I've always wanted an iPhone. Can we take photos of Bobby Deol's biceps on Tuesday? I hope he doesn't have security. I have to send it to Varsha.' See how young India is different. This girl Anjali, ugly and low class or whatever, but look at her dreams. iPhone. Photo with Bobby Deol. Proper ambitions. She'll do well in life.

'My boss said in one month I can buy a Santro,' said Ramesh, still trying to impress his father with his achievement.

'Good, because when I go to college now in our Maruti 800, kids throw stones at me. Most people don't even believe it's a car,' said Anjali with a toss of her hair.

I agree with Anjali. Maruti is not a car—it's mostly a trolley.

'Then I'm going to buy us a three-bedroom flat in Malad, papa. I've seen the building. Lakhotia Hercules. I got a leaflet too.'

'This is a church, beta.'

'Right now, it's a heritage church, papa, but the builders are hopeful of destroying it. See, a gym will come up here, a jacuzzi there…'

'What's wrong with this building, Ramesh? I got it approved by the central government.'

'Dad, our flat always smells of urine because we live next to a canal filled with urine. Did the central government approve the urine?' said Anjali.

I should explain that this is where Ramesh's sister went to her bedroom and came back wearing what I thought was a tribal warfare outfit. I had once seen something like this on National Geographic. But sometimes—seldom—I can be wrong. Unlike the accused in our Telecom scam, I am strong enough to admit it.

'What is that that you are wearing? Where are you going?'

For the first time, Old had a point.

'A few college girls were selected by DJ Bhooka Rascal to attend the MTV Bacardi Blast Kapre Utaro Party.'

'Your dress looks like you haven't paid for the whole thing. It's two-sevenths of a swimming costume.'

'Papa, I think what Anjali's wearing is called a boob tube.'

'What?'

'A boo…'

'I heard you, Ramesh. I am just surprised you would use a word like "boob" with your father socasually. Young people nowadays have no morals or shame.'

'People who say that are just jealous that they are too old to go to nightclubs,' said Anjali.

That's why I'm like Anjali. I go to nightclubs. My wife Antara used to say, 'It's a Monday night, why are you going to Club Enigma alone? There won't be anyone there.'

She missed the point. Yes, it was often empty, sometimes closed but the point was going out. I club. That's the message I was sending out. I'm not old. You know, here's an important business lesson—in any company you will find people who don't get your point of view. Don't marry them.

'Anjali, if you dress like this, how do you expect any positive responses on Shaadi.com?'

'Dad, maybe you should stop using Aishwarya Rai's photo and use mine instead.'

'Your actual photo got three responses from registered members of the Taliban.'

'Anjali, don't agree to an arranged marriage,' pleaded Ramesh.

'You stay out of this, Ramesh. Left to you, you will outsource her marriage to China.'

'Don't listen to dad. The only way our family can be happy is if Americans commit suicide. Bye.'

'Finish your...she's gone. Eh, Ramesh, I put an ad in today's *Times Matrimonials*. Here! Fair-skinned Hindu Girl, Brahmin government family, twenty-one centimetres tall seeks...'

'Papa, there's a typo. Twenty-one centimeters is three inches!'

'Oh. That's not very tall.'

I should explain here that Ramesh's sister was moving in and out of rooms. In the end, she was wearing lipstick, jewellery, and other things like that. I think her attempt was beauty. The attempt was laudable but like all ambitious efforts—Enron with Dhabol's power plant for example—it failed.

She rushed to her laptop.

'Shit. The party has started. You and Ramesh delayed me dad. Shit, shit, shit...where's my laptop...'

I'm usually quick to pick up on things but I had no idea what this woman was doing.

'What is going on here?'

Second good point raised by Old. He's getting cleverer with time. Like Single Malt.

'It could be online, papa.'

That's what I like about Ramesh. When faced with a problem, he's full of solutions. That's what you need in business. Solvers. There's no shortage of complainers but solvers solve things.

'What could be online?'

Now Old was back to being slow with information. This is why I won't hire anyone above fifty. There will be sparks of experience or whatever but soon, they will go back to talking rubbish. I've heard that no one on the Google Board of Directors is above forty. Perhaps because once someone explains a party can be an online party, they won't ask stupid questions like what could be online.

'There was an article I read in Rediff where people go to this DJ's website, log onto Skype and party. DJ Nikhil's site. Nikhil's DJ name is Bhooka Rascal. I didn't know it's tonight. I've never done it. I am seeing it for the first time.'

'So she doesn't go anywhere? Anjali are you going anywhere? Are you taking the car? ANJALI! See, I can't get her to respond.'

'Maybe everyone just comes online. My boss says in the future, everything will be online.'

'I'm going to Sharma Uncle's to play bridge. I have no idea what's happening to the world or my family,' said Old, exasperated by his children.

India is happening, negro! Wake up. That's what I would say if I was there. But I wasn't.

'Sssh, both of you!'

'We need to be quiet, dad. Anjali can't hear the DJ.'

Ugly Anjali, dressed like Naga warrior aside, was on top of something. And that something is what I call tech savvy. If you are stuck in the Amazon surrounded by piranhas, the difference between just savvy and tech savvy is everything. Just savvy, you die. Tech savvy, you live. It's the same with business.

She was laptop clubbing. Niche in India but with potential. I need to get into that scene.

How to speak American

In any job, training is key. Can you think of a plumber showing up to repair your toilet and not knowing what urine is? You'll throw him out immediately. It's the same thing with chartered accountancy or accents.

When my people call, I want the suicidees to not just feel like they are talking someone in the US, I want them to feel like they are listening to their own voice. As if someone is sitting on their lap whispering things to them. And when they wonder, who is it... who is it...they'll realize oh, it's them. This is the future of outsourcing. A lot of companies are trying to create a face-to-face feeling in the calls. I am trying to create a *face-on-face* feeling. I've even applied for a patent on that idea with the US Patent office.

So I hired some of the best accent trainers I could get. No, they are not from Harvard or Rosetta Stone or whatever other rackets are going around that these people at Infosys or 24/7 BPO are using. I used *real* people. People I met over there when I went on my extended research trip for a week—the same trip where I used up 23 percent of the capital given to me for the home appliances BPO, but let's not get into that right now. Read *Polyester Prince*. Even Dhirubhai made mistakes.

Here's the thing though. No one can do better accents than real people. That's my theory. And it's also another important lesson—real is better than something you can't afford.

My trainers came in on a Monday. I got a package deal from Sea Princess hotel. I'll explain later how. Breakfast and lunch the hotel would pay for. Dinner, I organized for them—Bhola cooked at home. My net outflow—two thousand rupees. Show me a BPO that can get its people trained in two thousand rupees. As Al Gore says in the documentary *Inconvenient Truths*, 'If you can't conserve, how will you earn?' He says that about the environment but I think it can be easily applied to suicide hotline accent training.

My office became the training room. That way I didn't need another room in the business centre called training room. These so-called training rooms are a scam anyway. They look like any other room and cost four thousand rupees an hour. If you're reading this, fuck you Prestige Business Centre. And especially you Mr Longines. How can you not include parking?

Anyway, I had hired the trainers only for thirty-six hours, so we started early, at 6 am. Well, to be honest, the training part was only five hours. They flew in by Air India (cheapest on baazi.com) at 4 am and their flight back was 6 pm. When I say I "had" them for thirty-six hours, it includes flying. You may say, which insane person will fly for sixteen hours to be in India for four hours, just for a free dinner and a stipend of three hundred dollars? To which I say one word, 'recession' or three words 'subprime mortgage crisis'. That may be four words.

I started the introductions. 'Listen up, fuckers. These Americans are your accent coaches. For the next few hours, they are going to be your mother, father, husband, jyotshi, dildo…everything. Whatever they say, you cram the information. If you can't, then go home and cram. After seven days if you can't speak like them, there is no point speaking at all. At the end of today if they tell me that you're not white, that you're still saying "what ya, no ya", and still sound like Shakti Kapoor, I'll either cut off your balls or your tongue. It'll be your choice.'

There was silence in the room. I wanted to set the ground rules so we knew what the rules were but maybe I pushed it too far too soon. I broke my own rule which I hadn't mentioned. So I decided to lighten the tone a bit. Maybe start with a joke.

'I'm just kidding. This is not Slumdog. We are ISO certified.'

'Okay, I'll do the introductions first. I'm Brad,' said the man sitting uncomfortably on my desk.

'No. I will. I'm Arun Gupta. People, these are *live* Americans. This is Brad. He is a failed actor. That is Anne. She is a failed nun. They will teach you how to speak.'

'Um, nuns don't fail, Mr Gupta. I went to a seminary,' Anne interjected.

'Um...okay...I'm Brad, I'm from New York City, which is this little dot on the right in the middle of this really tiny map of the USA. You all get that this is the US of A right? Right?' Brad pointed it out on a map of Mexico.

Bhola had gotten the wrong map but it didn't matter. USA was on it. Small, but on it.

I got it going. As the CEO, you have to.

'Good, now say, "Hi Brad".' Now Brad got going.

'Hi, Bread,' said Ramesh.

'Eh bastard, Ramesh, he's not a loaf, he's a person.'

'Hi, Brid.'

'Darling, Rashmi, he's not a car.'

'Bra...raaa...open your mouth wide...say raaa... aaaa.' Good. Brad was taking charge.

'Aaaaa...'

'You have to open your mouths to speak. We Americans are very clear when we...'

'Braaaaaa...'

'Speak. Thank you, Mr Ramesh. Great, now a quick show of hands. How many here have ever been to the US?'

I obviously put up my hand. Been there, done dat. I misspelt that on purpose. You can do that kind of cool stuff when you know the right spelling. It's like wearing torn jeans.

'Okay, not a problem. Through my class, you'll feel you're there. We'll go on an accent road trip from Seattle to Tampa—do you all know what a road trip is?'

'No one here has a car. They hang from trains,' I pointed out. I felt like I had to give them a lesson in Indian economics. I would expect trainers to have read Thomas Friedman but given how poor everyone is over there now, books may be out. But it didn't matter because Rashmi jumped in.

'Yes, it is on Route 66. It is a highway. I have worked for a call centre on USA driving directions.'

'See, I told you she's my bitch. Well done, Rashmi.'

'Okay, Mr Arun, you're a little bit out of line here with bad language. Okay, I'm Sister Anne and I have a question. What if a customer, I'll call them customers, uses bad language? What do you do then?'

'We will use better language.'

'No, I mean what if they use language to swear, young man, like Arun just did.'

'Like if they say fuck you and all? Bloody bastard, bloody asshole, Indian son of a bitch—I'll come over there cut your balls off. That kind of thing?'

I was surprised by Ramesh's anger. Then I realized why.

'I used to work in HSBC Home Loans. I know.'

'Yes. Like that. But Jesus wouldn't like you using language like that, and remember, all Americans love Jesus.'

'Don't entirely believe her. Not all.'

That was said by the homo Brad.

When I hired them, it didn't strike me but now I knew. Nun Anne and Homo Brad were very different from each other. Conservative versus Liberal. Bush versus Obama. Red versus Blue. Sometimes a state can be a red or blue state. That refers to the levels of terrorist threat. So if an MSNBC (that's a channel over there) says, 'Virginia has voted blue', it means Virginia has voted for fewer terrorist acts. That's an important business lesson—always know your market—politics, society, everything.

I thought two Americans would get along but I suppose if you believe in different things and if you've had a fourteen-hour, non-stop Air India flight in the last row of economy next to a toilet on a very turbulent flight, you will fight. I hadn't foreseen that. And in business, foreseeing is almost better than seeing. Their fight had something to do with gulab jamun. I think the nun stole the homo's sweet or maybe it was the other way round. Or maybe it was the chicken bhuna supreme. I don't know why they don't save the food and eat it later. That's the whole point of the aluminium foil. That's why I hate airline food on airlines. That's why I eat it at home.

'Okay, so if there was a customer like that, how will you handle it?'

My Rashmi took the lead.

'I'll say this to them, "I understand your frustration, sir, but can you please explain to us the circumstances under which you have thought about ending your life".'

'Very good. Have you done this before?'

'Yes, I've been in the call centre industry almost five years and I've read your manual, *What is America?*'

'Excellent, you've read my book. She's read my book. What's your name?'

I had no idea that the failed nun had also written some accent book. That's the thing about Americans. They do random things. I once met this stripper, Candice, who was also interning at the UN. It's called multi-tasking. And they have so many of these *Chicken Soup for the Soul* type things. Self-improvement. This must be like that—for accents.

'Rashmi, but here I am Meghan, sister. Always Meghan.'

'And where are you from, Meghan?'

'Good question, nun.'

It was a good question. I had to point it out.

'Pensacola, Florida. My brother, Baxter, is a marine.'

'Yes! Nice! You go, bitch!' I always reward good performance. She had invented a brother called Baxter. Even better.

'Good. Okay, who am I? Like I said, I'm Brad. I'm a writer-performer-dancer-poet and I live in the West Village, which is this really beautiful, creative temple in the heart of Manhattan. I live with my boyfriend, Jeff, who's a wonderful potter. I was in this Off Broadway play where I play this...this really interesting Indian vegetable that transforms into Vishnu, your God, and after a show, I met your CEO, Arun, who is really sweet, very wealthy. He loved my part, and...'

'Hurry up, man, I'm paying for your time here.'

Honestly, I don't remember meeting Brad. It was raining and I needed some place before my Starbucks meeting. Starbucks coffee was three dollars, this play nonsense was free. So I went in. They were doing some crazy acting in there, and later they told me it was written by some guy called Ionescyo. Probably Japanese. I don't understand all these theatre types. But I could guess all of them were homos. That's also important in business—understanding the sexual preference of your customer. If your customer, say, is dead, it's pointless selling him life insurance, no? These things are important to pick up.

'Where was I? So yes, he hired me to come to Mumbai to spend a day with you wonderful people to teach you how Americans communicate. So today, as our first lesson we are going to work as a team to remove your native-tongue interferences, so that when you speak English, you do so clearly. I want to make sure we understand you when we call you.'

'Excuse, I have question. When you say you live with that boyfriend, are you saying you are a homo man?'

'Um. Yes, Mr Ramesh, yeah, I am gay. That's correct. We don't call people "homo man" where I'm from because that's considered disrespectful.'

'When we start work, will we have to help homos when they do suicide?'

'I'm hoping you'll have to help anyone who calls. It's a Suicide Hotline. You have no right to discriminate against a person's sexual preference.'

'Sir, why?'

I needed to clarify something here. 'Eh, gays are also people. First, they are paying customers. Second, they are homos. In the US, there are all kinds of psychos.'

'Oh, Okay. Sorry, sir.'

Nun Anne began, 'Okay boys and girls, I've written some American terms here for your reference. I don't use this language in church but I see young people using it. Gs, like I have to spend 40 Gs, usually refers to money. Dog, as in "what up dog?" means "hello". Dog is a term for friend.'

'Or bitch…for women friend.' When you have knowledge of something, don't be shy to share it, that's what I say.

'Actually, Mr Arun, the friendly term is "biatch". As in "what up biatch?" It's different from "bitch", which is considered an insult. It's tricky. For example, a teenager might say "chilling", which means "resting".'

No nun can keep me down.

'Or for example "chillax", sister, when I combine "chilling" and "relaxing". Write that down, you both.'

'Don't write that down. So, Meghan, tell us… what are the key values of America that I talk of in my book?'

'In her book, Madam Anne says that America's key values are, as George W. Bush also says, almighty

God Jesus, marriage, family values, individuality, financial success…'

'She forgot one—pursuit of happiness. Madam, I have not read this book but I know the main goals of the US. Last night there was a Stevan Segal movie on Zee Studio called *Save America*. They mentioned it over there. I remembered.'

'Thank you, Greg. Meghan, now you know my country?' asked the nun.

'Okay, Anne's America is not my America. In my America, Barack Obama's America, there are divorced people, same sex partners, atheists, people who hate their parents, and 70 percent of my country is single,' said Brad.

'Sinners like Mr Brad are going to burn in hell. They are also called liberals. They live in the East and West coasts and are the work of the devil,' Anne bit through her words.

I jumped in with a new business idea. I call it ATOPO—Always Thinking of Potential Opportunities. 'Maybe they will try to kill themselves, so we have a captive base of customers. Write down, target market—atheist homos.'

But that bloody Brad kept fighting. Luckily, it was in his US accent so technically, he was training also.

'At least I don't sexually abuse children, I don't manufacture misconceptions about Darwinian evolution, and I don't go to gay bath houses while my wife waits with dinner and the kids!'

I thought of another ATOPO.

'Write down, target market—pervert priests.'

'You're a fag, Brad.'

'Nazi Anne.'

'Girly Boy Brad.'

'Paedophile Anne.'

They continued fighting. I cancelled their dinner voucher. Whatever Bhola cooked, I ate over the next three days. Was it a bit of a crisis? Yes. But in every crisis, there is opportunity.

'You guys, observe how Americans fight. There will be a lot of shouting and screaming when your customers call. Take notes, take notes!'

See what I did there? I made it look like the fighting was part of the training.

Thinking on your feet is key to business. Some businesses only think on their feet, like if you run a security company. Tops Security for example. I know the CEO, Ronit Roy. He's a rubbish actor in a serial. *Husbands ke Chote Chote Sapne*. Rubbish serial. I told him that. Once when I was passing his car on the Mumbai-Pune Expressway, I said, 'Hey, you, Rohit Roy, you're shit.' He hit me.

I don't watch soaps so I can't tell you that his character, Vemlu Dewan, got a promotion at Yes Bank. Okay, maybe I have seen one or two or fifty-six episodes. Thing is, most offices are nine to five. I work five to nine. If you don't know what that is, it's night. It's not my fault that there's nothing else on Viacom Colors in the morning.

It didn't matter that he hit me in the face. He took me to Wockhardt Panvel. I respect that. I also respect that when he is sitting in his trailer learning the shit script for *Husbands Ke*... he is thinking, how can I get more of my security guards to guard more Mumbai buildings? That's two jobs boss—dual as they say. When you have that kind of a double role, it doesn't matter if you break my nose. The actor Omar Sharif was a world famous Bridge player. Again, like Ronit Roy, double role.

The point is not whether my training session broke into a fight between the nun and Brad where employees from Cairn Energy next door had to come and break it up. Point is, at the end of it all, were Ramesh and Rashmi trained in American? They were. At TCS, they get months to do this and they call it employee orientation. It took me only four hours, Air India, and one fist fight.

Every minute spent breathing is lost business

I'm going with my whole ATOPO thing, if you still remember that key business phrase, and looking for opportunities everywhere. And you have to travel for it. Bhola's father died last week and even though I knew there would be no Americans at his thing in Ghatkopar, only servants and whateverrr, I didn't turn off my switch. I surveyed. Scoped. That's very important when you have your own business—you can never have an off button. Just ask Anand Mahindra. He tweets at 4 am. While he's asleep.

Three days had passed since nun and homo filed that FIR that I bribed Sub-Inspector Holkar to squash but most importantly, my people were trained. The call centre business is like the restaurant business. No point buying fresh rice and milk and meat if no one is eating. Rashmi and Ramesh were my inventory. Stocked and ready. Now I needed people outside to feed. Paying customers. Otherwise, like all perishables, they would perish. Just look what happened to Salt Water Grill on Chowpatty Beach.

So from my capital base, I'd spent a little on the fucking business centre, which I like to call Mandatory Crap Infrastructure Cost (my own accounting term), because employees need to sit or whatever, a little on the trainers (where I cleverly saved a hundred dollars on dinner and made it personal expenses, ie, my dinner). But now there was a big expense—going to the US.

Cheapest on rediff.com that day was Lufthansa. I had no choice; I had to sort out how we'd get paid. It's fine for people to say, 'Oh Arun, you're a genius, you outsourced suicide helplines', but just like discovering the Internet or how to fly, you have to figure out how to make money. Otherwise, it's nothing. Like the guy who invented the Hoopla; where is he now? Compared to say, the CEO of British Airways or Netscape. So that's the main thing. Cash. And I had to spend to go there to figure out how the cash would get here.

I was already seated when she slid into the seat next to me. She looked tired because of the thing she did to wrap herself in the blanket. It's a tactic to show your fellow passenger, 'Oh, I'm ready to get some sleep after this long India trip'. And maybe she was tired buying some crap Adivasi earrings or sarongs or a sadhu mattress and things like that these white people buy. But the thing is, I know my business. The rest of the plane could see a hot blonde in a T-shirt that said 'Barcelona Asian Film Festival'. But do you know what I saw? A customer.

You know what else? I smelt her perfume. Chanel. I do my research, boss. What do you think? I don't know Heathrow or the ground floor of Selfridges? I recognize smells. Put it all together. What I'm trying to say is that I recognize the difference between someone who is just a person (useless) and someone who is a Potential Revenue Generator (PRG). And another important lesson is this—when you see a PRG, jump on it/him/her/them.

'Hello.'

'Hi.'

'Going to America?'

'Sorry?'

'Going to the US? By flight?'

'Yes. This is a non-stop flight to New York, so yes.'

'Nice. Super. Me also. Going to break out revenue streams, growth projections...you won't understand. I'm Arun Gupta. You?'

'Jennifer Roberts.'

'Hi Jennifer. Nice name. Some could call you Jen, some Iffer. So people call you what?'

'Jennifer.'

In a sales situation, never sell your product. Always try to make your customer feel comfortable. Talk about all sorts of things, interests, politics, views... you know, all that crap till you jump on your prey. If you don't know what I'm talking about, watch any shark special on the Discovery Channel.

'Happy?'

'Huh?'

'Generally, in life.'

'Sorry?'

'As in, you aren't depressed or anything?'

'No. Why?'

'Nothing. Never thought about killing yourself?'

'Look, I really don't know where this conversation is going.'

'You should.'

'I'd like to move my seat.'

'Consider everything though. You're pretty ugly. No wedding ring. So single. Probably live alone with what, a dog? Cat? Some old mother?'

'You're an asshole.'

'Look, please seriously consider why your life is total shit and why you've wasted whatever opportunities life gave you to reach this pathetic, mediocre, miserable place where you're sitting next to me in the economy class of a Lufthansa flight in your middle age. And why no one loves you.'

That's what is called the sales pitch climax.

'I'm going to fucking hurt you.'

'And then when you're ready to do something to yourself, like hang from a fan, or buy a gun, or put your head in the oven, call this number.'

Sometimes a pitch goes well and you immediately know. You know because the customer tells you. Sometimes you don't find out for years. This one didn't go all that well. How do I know? She slapped me. But am I embarrassed? No. I mean, I'm writing about it two years later so how can I be? And I'm Arun Gupta, do you see embarrassed anywhere in the spelling? No is the answer. Okay, did she call the Air Marshall so that I was detained for three hours at JFK airport and interrogated? Yes. I'll admit it, I have no probs. In all this though, you know what the main thing is—I tried. That's business boss, always failing. Think of it as climbing Everest. You do everything to get up there and realize it's not there or you've accidentally climbed Kilimanjaro. So now you have to go back down and try all over again. That's everyday in the business world.

This Iffer may be angry with me now but I slid my crumpled business card into her Prada bag. She will think about what I said and someday will call. You watch.

Many hours later, I met the real suicide hotline people in Florida. Don't ask me about the connecting flight bag check-in charge. Nowadays the fuckers charge fifteen dollars for every checked-in bag. That's almost Ramesh's salary. Forget that. I sat with the bag on my lap. What is more important? My bag checked-in or Ramesh still employed to receive your call when you are dying?

Sarah had set up the meeting. It was near Cape Canaveral which is some place that has this massive golf ball. I miss the point of it. Sometimes I can understand why Americans want to die. They have all this crazy shit. You've just lost your job, you're driving home trying to figure out how to tell your wife and kids that your home is on subprime mortgage or whatever and you are driving past this giant golf ball. It would make anyone mad.

So these suicide ladies were nice. They were also old. And business is not about old. It's about...yes, young. So I did most of the talking. They couldn't understand what I was saying so they didn't understand that in five years, their Suicide Watch or whatever the fuck would all be 1888 Dial India.

They got only seven dollars an hour, and they couldn't understand the point of this being outsourced to India. They kept making some totally irrelevant point saying they saved lives of Americans who needed comfort or some shit, but I said boss, people are people. Comfort is comfort, uniform across hemispheres and latitudes. Life and death are universal. So what if it's a man in San Francisco dying and you are sitting in Cape Canaveral talking to him. You can sit in Prestige Business Centre and do the same thing at one-fourth the cost. In fact, if you went somewhere cheaper than Prestige, you could probably do it at one-seventh the cost (which I think is less than one-fourth but I haven't done the math).

The main thing in business is the main thing everywhere—keeping costs down. There are some ladies in Florida that run this thing—Suicide Watch. It is America's main suicide hotline but these ladies are fools; no MBAs, just three chicks called Anne, Jane, and Margaret. All above 60. Not even in suits. They have some psychology degree or some shit and are running this for charity like an NGO. Making losses. Unbelievable. This must be the same as when the Europeans discovered that the new world had no system of land ownership. How can someone not own land? How can you not monetize suicide? Same thing.

These Florida ladies near this golf ball place are costing this suicide hotline thirty thousand dollars a year to operate. Plus phone bills. Plus absentees. Plus old. Plus benefits, coffee machine, chit chat about grandchildren crap. I am doing this at five thousand. The word is arbitrage. That's real business. It's like making the iPhone for three dollars and selling it for four hundred. Another word—China. And in the context of Chinese manufacturing, a third word—respect. They are so dedicated at keeping manufacturing costs down that they refuse to learn English. English would mean wasting time talking to each other. They understand that in international business, silence=productivity. That's why respect.

Honestly, if it's the old ladies versus me, the old ladies don't stand a chance. But look, I am not heartless like Ajmal Kasab. I have a heart. I am not saying give me all the phone lines. I will start with one, prove myself, and then you can give me the whole thing and turn this place into a basketball court or whatever sport these people are into.

One phone line at a time. One save at a time. Then slowly climb to greater heights, like Aamir Khan or Narayan Murthy. And I worked out the revenue stream because that's the most critical thing ever in any business. Otherwise you can end up like those fools, what are they called, scientists. Coming up with clean energy, flying, changing liquid rocket crystal ethanol…whatever the fuck they come up with, but they make no money from it. Not even for a hair cut. So I would get paid thus—every save would give me one dollar. Every death, zero. The client would dial into this same number here, which is a paid 1-888 number similar to my blow job and appliance line etc, but it would be rerouted to me through Cisco (Sarah organized that through her husband; free sex was payment through her marriage vows…I didn't need to make any new payments).

When I was leaving, someone asked me a stupid question. They said, 'Well, if the number is 1888 Dial India, won't the callers realize their call is being routed to India?'

I responded, 'Duh. Details.'

Honestly, in business sometimes people don't see the bigger picture. What's important is the number. 1-888-534-6195. No one, especially dying people, look at the letters.

Notes from battle

Once I got back from that not-happening country to the happening country, I got into action.

Just to explain the level of not happening, I go to the airport for my flight back and they have me on some 'no-fly list'. I tell them, if I am on your 'no-fly list', how did I fly here? No answer. 'How was I detained by Air Marshalls for that Iffer thing?' No answer. Then they said that was a different airline. Yes, it was but it still flew, was my argument. Apparently, they have me on some database of Interpol and I thought, whoa, clearly the Maharashtra tax issue could not have...but then they said sorry sorry, they meant Harun Gupta also known as Harun Gupta Khan. Now, I am also known by other names—most distinguished people are—but not that one. Harun Gupta, they told me later, was dead. That's how they knew it wasn't me. So yes, spending three hours in an airport interrogation room with various large black people can be seen by some as intimidating. To me, it was a business idea. The homeland security databases need to be updated. For starters, take dead people off the plane.

Once I was happening again, by which I mean when I had landed, I was moving. Some people don't move till the plane stops. Some people don't get off till everyone in the plane has gotten off. How can you wait that long? In a country on the move, you cannot stand still.

The difference is simple. Remember Rajesh Khanna? Great actor, Nehru jacket wearing, teen heart throb, always dying in 70's romcom movies? Back then, when he walked outside his bungalow in Bandra, Indira Gandhi had to declare an emergency. The newspapers were banned from writing anything. Read about 70's Indian history, you will know. Back then, he was on the move. Then he stopped. Today he spends all day walking outside his bungalow in Bandra and the country functions normally. Nothing is declared by the PM. *The Times of India* continues unaffected. Someone told me it's not even his bungalow. He walks around other people's houses. Someone else said he's bought a dog but no one could confirm. That's the punishment of standing still when the country moves on. You become a pet owner but are no longer a home owner.

Compare that to Mr Amitabh Bachchan. He kept moving. When the Indian telecom revolution happened, he bought his first cell phone. Today, when the Indian telecom industry is a 50 billion market, he has four cell phones. When new shampoos and suits were introduced, he used them and advertised them. He's kept up with the times. That's why he still can't leave his bungalow without at least one press person dying in a stampede. And that's why he now has four bungalows. As Juhu was redeveloped, so was he. Always in motion.

This is new India. Standing equals retired homeless dog owner. Movement equals Amitabh Bachchan. That's the world change explained in two sentences.

Before we got our first chance, there was some further negotiation. I land and I get an email from those Old Florida ladies saying, 'Your behaviour was atrocious. You are a mad man.' I immediately knew what they were really trying to say. Bring down the price of my commission per saved life. I went back with several counter offers, but nothing. I was beginning to think they were tough negotiators, almost like a Gujrati diamond merchant in Antwerp who will think twice before a .0003 percent discount. They did not respond at all. I was running out of counter strategies for crazy Florida women, when luck, a huge factor in business, sent me the following message:

> Dear Mr Gupta,
>
> I think you were talking to my grandmother Margaret Jackson about her suicide hotline. It was really a voluntary service never meant to be a business. She passed away last night and none of her family is involved in this venture.

I believe you came to see the women with some business idea. Please call me.

Thanks,
Normal Jackson (her son)
Assistant Coach (under 15s)
Nick Bolletierri Tennis Academy
Orlando, Florida.

I know what you're thinking. Hell yeah! Did I jump? Okay, yes. Normally I don't celebrate death. You shouldn't. But this. Hell yeah.

Fresh negotiations and we were rolling. Getting your first customer is always the hardest. Everyone from Ford to Pepsi to Ikea will tell you that. But getting your first customer because their parent died and left you a business opportunity…that's something else entirely.

And yes, like I said before, I was lucky because of this bereavement. But was Spain lucky when they found a mine with all of South America's gold in it? Yes. Were Chinese companies happy when they got massive tax breaks to compete with American products? Yes. Granted, no old ladies were required to die for those businesses to boom but luck did play a factor. The same thing happened here.

One of the main things people don't think about when starting an outsourcing business is the phone. That's the bread and butter of calling. Without the phone, you are at a slight disadvantage. It's like Reliance without petroleum. There would be nothing to rely on them for. So I bought two new phones. Samsung XJENBX2. Best equipment in town. If these babies can't save Americans, nothing can. Yes, I know what you're thinking. Additional expense. But whateverrr.

I kept a log of the calls. I didn't know that someday I would write a book and put it in word for word, but funny how life is. I think, without the calls, it is impossible to write a motivational business book about a call centre. Of course there is confidentiality. I'm not a fool. I have not put in the customers' home addresses, just their names and their mental condition. No issues with the ones that died. Lesser chances of a lawsuit.

Call Log

Time: 1:30 am
Date: October 23, 2008
Duration: 3.23 minutes.

'This is Terence. Who am I speaking with?'

'911, this is Meghan. Are you near any firearms or sharp objects? Do you have access to poisons, toxins, or home appliances that can harm you?'

'Um...no.'

'How can I help you, sir?'

'I just got laid off, Meghan.'

'Okay...I'm very sorry to hear that, sir. How long have you been having sexual issues?'

'No, what? Oh, not laid, laid off…let go from my job.'

The trainer should have covered that difference. There is a fine difference between laid and laid off. Something like Caesar chicken, which is a salad, and Caesar, Julius, who was a king and Caesar's Palace, the casino. Not a lot of people know that. But I do, and now by reading me, they do. And among them is you. So you do too. It's like this amazing thing I saw in Dubai—a large sea world inside a mall with dolphins and sharks and turtles. And in front of it, GAP. Now normally, you wouldn't put khakis and deep sea fish together. But when you do, people think 'Oh, this' and then 'this also'. Very similar. Anyway, back to problem.

'I used to work in data systems and my boss, Thomas, was a friend of mine. He was British. He got laid off too. They're shifting my whole team, all the servers, to India, to this company called Satyam data systems. Do you know what that is?'

'Satyam Infoway, taking India to the world. Yes sir. I have seen TV advertisements.'

'Where are you? You sound really weird. What's your deal?'

'Sir, is there an emergency I can help you with?'

'I'm in Manhattan. I'm on 73rd and Amsterdam. I'm about to walk into Food Emporium. Do you have that where you are?'

'I'm in Florida, sir. Great weather all year round, and how about those Tampa Bay Buccaneers?'

Local football team reference. I taught her that. It's like the Kolkata Knight Riders of Tampa Bay. Throwing that in makes her more authentic.

'What? Are you talking about football? I'm talking about grocery.'

'Sir, the most famous mall in Florida is...'

'So here's the deal okay—I'm going to buy some artichokes, some mushrooms, and some chicken broth to make a soup, and then I'm going to walk home. I live on a third floor walk-up on 75th and Amsterdam. It's nice. We went to southern Italy and we bought these plates of wood, for salads and stuff, and I have some Toulouse Lautrec posters from Paris, rugs from Istanbul, stuff we've collected, you know. It's a two-bedroom apartment but with our life's belongings, travel souvenirs, novels, you know.'

At Wharton case studies, this is known as the introduction to the problem.

'You seem to be a rich man, sir. Rich is better than poor.'

'Yeah. Ha ha. It is. So I pay four thousand a month rent. My wife doesn't work—she teaches kids to sing. Third graders, minority kids in the Bronx, they pay her a hundred bucks a lesson. She takes the 1 pm train. I have two sons Jeremy and Harry, in third and seventh grade. They go to a fancy school on the Upper West Side. Young British women from Cambridge teach them. Their school costs, together, sixty thousand a year, plus classical music lessons. Harry learns karate at this camp in Maine. I spend a hundred grand on them. Not to mention international family holidays, trips to my parents in Chicago. Kate likes shoes by Miu Miu—I think it's some expensive Prada thing—more expensive than regular designer stuff because they've stopped making Bangladeshi children stitch it. We hold season tickets to Lincoln Center. Kate's my wife—what do you think of all this?'

Analysis of the problem. Terence either does not like his wife's shopping or his son's karate. Was Rashmi getting that? Suicide hotlines are like T20 matches. You can't tell how and when the run rate climbs. The problem was climbing. I wasn't sure she was getting that.

'You are a lucky man, sir, to have such a nice family. America is wonderful to raise a family and live in peace.'

'What I'm trying to tell you, Meghan, is that it costs me over two hundred and fifty thousand dollars to just survive. And I have a month's severance. And I have no savings.'

Okay, no, that was the problem.

'That is not good, sir.'

'All the head-hunters I called told me it's the worst recession they've ever seen. I don't have a college degree. In the seventies, I got into data management. It is just what I got into. I dropped out of Ithica College and joined IBM. It made sense then.'

'IBM is multinational. Good choice.'

'And the cosmopolitan opportunities my family has are all big city things; I can't move upstate or to De Moines—there won't be people like us.'

'Sir, have you thought about yoga?'

Good, small talk, good. Small talk buys the customer time. More importantly, they buy time from us. Also, they get distracted. I had not trained her on this but the best distraction is saying something like 'I am totally naked right now'. They don't expect that. In Rashmi's case, she went with yoga. Same destination, different journey.

'Meghan, shut the fuck up please and listen to me. What I'm trying to tell you is that I love my family. My wife is a good woman, she's kind and beautiful and we laugh at Christopher Guest films, and my children are erudite and can make Japanese aperitifs and hold their own in a conversation on Apple technology or organic farming. We are model urban globalized godless Americans—we travel, we read, we haven't inherited much, we explore ideas and cultures, we own nothing, we drink wine, we talk of David Sedaris and moderate Islam…'

'You are the best, sir.'

'But I'm going to go home now, Meghan, and if I don't find them at home—which I know I won't—I'm going to make this soup. I'm going to drink this soup. And then I'm going to drown myself. What do you think of that, Meghan?'

Okay, finally, there was the problem. Financial. Unlike me, clearly he had not invested in tax free HSBC FMPs.

'Sir, your family will not like that.'

'They might. There's some insurance. Not enough.'

'Sir, a single suicide is equal to ten murders to the ones you leave behind.'

'Are you reading from a website or something?'

'Sir, please don't do it.'

'Meghan, I'm not calling to ask your permission. I'm calling to tell you that my wife's cell phone number is 347-887-2121. She won't be able to get back in because I would be in the bathroom and she didn't take her keys. So call her and tell her what's happened. Will you do that for me?'

'We cannot do outgoing calls, sir.'

'Oh, that's a bummer.'

'Arun sir, what is bummer?' she said, as an aside.

Obviously, I knew. It's a large car—the Americans use it in Iraq. I told her so.

'Sir, you have a bummer? You can start by selling the bummer—it is a big car, good money.'

'What? What I'm trying to say is how is she going to get into the house? It's a bummer, as in a problem.'

Sometimes Americans don't know their own words. I can't help illiteracy. I donate to NGOs; that's the most I can do.

'Sir, what is your favourite thing to cook?' Rashmi continued patiently.

Honestly, I thought she had gone mad. Too much stress on her first call.

'Um…I make a really good roast. Beef.'

'Tell me the recipe. Please.'

I thought, disconnect before it gets worse but the customer was still talking so I didn't. I mean he had run out of money and Rashmi was teaching him how to make a steak. This was not going to end well.

'Well you need a dead cow first, great cut of meat…'

'And the shop you are in has that?'

'Oh yeah, this place has great cuts.'

'Will you go and check?'

'I'm in front of the meat place.'

'You like?'

'Yeah, today's is really fresh. I know the butcher, Tariq. He just waved to me. He's from Lebanon I think. I've bought meat here for years.'

'Carry on…'

'I don't like spices a lot, so just a light marinating, salt and sugar maybe, just a touch of red wine, little pepper. The temperature is key…I'm getting hungry now that I'm talking about this…'

'And what it is you like in liquor?'

'Oh you mean wine?'

'Yes, why not?'

'Shiraz is nice, some bits of Cabernet. In fact, I see a '97 I've been looking for for a while.'

'How will you eat and drink this pleasure when you are not alive?'

To be honest, I didn't understand what her strategy was. In fact, I didn't understand it for two days. On day three after this call, I woke up and realized what she had done. That's the thing in business sometimes—the element of surprise. And not getting it. Many things happen and you won't get it. It doesn't matter. You will eventually. The head of IBM didn't believe computers had a future. I was like him with this food tangent Rashmi went on about.

'I haven't thought about what I'm going to do, Meghan. That's why it's best to do it quickly.'

'Sir, can I beg you to do something? Can you smell fresh food? Please take in deep breath.'

'Okay…'

'What can you smell?'

'Some great foreign herb or something.'

'You like cooking with this herb?'

'Who doesn't? Like a stew. A beef stew would be great with herbs.'

'Sir, buy cow, salt, pepper, whatever. Take it home and make a great roast. Cook it slowly, with herb and meat and sauce. You have it with your great American family, and drink lots of wine. Then I am requesting you to please enjoy some coitus with your beloved Kate and then you call me in the morning. Ask for Meghan okay?'

'Umm…'

'Please. You are under lot of stress. If you do something in a hurry you will regret it, but you won't even be able to do that because you'll be dead.'

'What if I make a really good dinner and everyone loves it and I look around and realize I can't ever do this to the people I love so much?'

'Yes sir, what if?'

Brilliant. What a recovery. Better than Sachin against Pakistan in 2004 World Cup chasing 275, better than Tiger Woods if he ever made a comeback—actually better than Tiger Woods having a threesome—better than the return of the Congress in 2004 when everyone thought they had left India, better than Goldman Sachs bouncing back after being arrested, better than Jet Airways showing a profit of seven rupees after losses of seven crores. You don't need any more examples of what this is better than. It's better.

Call Log

Time: 3:45 am
Date: October 27, 2008
Duration: 2:50 minutes.

'Greg, are you there?'

'Lisa, how long have you been standing on Brooklyn Bridge?'

'An hour, maybe two.'

Bridge jumping case, fairly standard I thought. Till you see what happens. That's one thing in business—unpredictability. You just never know what happens next. It's not like life.

'And once again, your favourite writers you said are Edwin…'

'Edward…Edward Albee.'

'Yes, carry on…Thomas?'

'Tom Stoppard.'

'And you said two more.'

'David Mamet and Sam Shephard.'

Customer background information is good. Engaging the customer is good. Or so I thought. Sometimes when I am right, I can also be wrong. I don't know how it happens but it happened here.

'Excellent. Now what do you like about their dramatics?'

'Nothing. They are plays, not dramatics. Dramatics sounds…never mind.'

'And what has been your favourite part and in what?'

'Mother Courage. Bertold Brecht. It's a wonderful part.'

'See now, she had courage, this mother.' Ramesh put his hand on the microphone. Clearly an indication that he was drowning himself as this woman was jumping. 'Arun sir, entertainment expert hai koyi? I have an entertainment case. I need entertainment back-up and info jaldi. Broadway dancing and all. Jaldi. Anyway possible, sir?'

I told him one word—Google. Sometimes a word is all you need to sum up everything. Like Newton had a word—gravity.

'Hello? Greg?'

'Why else would they call her Mother Courage? Why don't you be like her? Why you have to do this killing yourself? That is not courage? That is what? Nothing.'

'Do you know how hard and insulting it is to audition day after day and keep up the appearance? How physically and emotionally impossible it all is? I can't eat. My smile, my words, my movement, all disingenuous…I'm not a person, I'm a thing.'

'Tell me about the audition please.'

'It always the fucking same. It always in the same fucking place. 43rd Street. A room with mirrors. That long cream table. Fake politesse. Some foreign theatre director with black glasses. I didn't get it.'

'Sir, I need a name of US actor.' He turned to me at this moment.

I am always there to back up my people. So I had a two-word answer this time. Amitabh Bachchan.

'Sir, Amitabh is Indian. How she will know?'

I could have told Ramesh to watch that CNN interview to see just how popular Amitabh is around the world—he even has a doctorate in Romania and New Zealand—but there was no time for that. By the time I would have explained his popularity and he translated that to the customer by sending links and *Filmfare* copies, Fed Ex would take at least four days. And she would not stand on the bridge for four days no matter what they say about dedicated actors. So I had to think of something for the moment. That's an important business lesson—deadlines. Deadlines, they say, can be life and death—like here. So I went with two other words. Gwyneth Paltrow.

'Gwy—okay…thank you, sir. Lisa, I would like to remind you about this Gwyneth Paltrow…she is an actress. She had a tough time a getting role. Today she is a star. She is there. And where are you? You are on a bridge giving up. How can you let this happen?'

'What? Don't tell me about Gwyneth Paltrow. Are you crazy telling me about Gwyneth Paltrow? What does that have to do with me? Stop telling me crazy things.'

'I am sorry. I am not the best maybe, at words. But I want to know, what is so wrong that jumping is the answer?'

'I am attractive. I have a 4.0 from Bryn Mawr. I've read Plato. I've studied *Theatre of Social Unrest*. I went to Actors Studio. I've lived in New York for ten years. I've eaten dry fruits for a month to save money, temped on Wall Street, done pest control, sold Amway. I have a hundred thousand dollars in unpaid loans. I thought I could fall in love and balance my financial situation but they leave me, and they mostly take my stuff. Whatever little fucking stuff I have. One Ferris Beuhler video, a little Sri Lankan lamp... how annoying is that? From my little Brooklyn studio, which is shit. Nothing. I haven't paid rent because I was seeing my landlord. Now, he's leaving me and selling the place to a gay Moroccan couple. What am I going to do? You tell me, what else am I supposed to do? What can I do?'

'Your father and mother? Where is the family? It is everything.'

'I don't speak to them. It's a long story.'

'Sir, kya karu?'

'Sorry, I don't understand you.'

'Madam, kuch worry ki baat nahi hain.'

'What?'

'Madam, please don't lose focus. That is nothing.'

'Were you speaking Hindi? Was that Hindi?'

'No, you are slowly going crazy and imagining things.'

'Are you in India? Is this call going to India? Don't fuck with me…I used to work for a helpdesk at American Airlines. Am I having this conversation with…'

'No, madam, no…I am a healthcare professional… certified healthcare…in the state of Pennsyl…madam? Please…hello! Fuck man…I'm Gregory…Greg…Go Pittsburg Steelers…madam? Shit. God.'

So there it is. There are two important lessons to be learnt here. The first, Ramesh is an idiot. The second, in life, there are no second chances. Elvis Presley said that. And when someone that big says something, it's worth listening to. It may have been Ramesh's first call but breaking into Hindi was as fatal a mistake as Hitler marching into a Russian winter in 1943, or Google Chrome. Sometimes, one is all it takes. Ask anyone who died of cancer.

Chillax time

Someone had once told me a story of a man who was so bored of his job that one day he came in, sat at his cubicle, drank his coffee, switched on his computer, and died. Just like that. Face flat on desk. Dead.

That story is often told in business circles as a lesson on how to motivate employees. They say, always give employees something exciting enough to do so they don't die. My take on this is different. After a tough day of work, take them clubbing. No one is ever bored in a club. Mainly because you can't hear yourself thinking. By the time your thoughts come to, Oh, I'm bored with my life, I hate my joint family, maybe I should…you are four shots down. Have you ever heard of anyone dying in a club of boredom? Yes, people die in clubs with gun shots but that's the opposite of boredom. That's things happening. Like last week, there was a shootout at Club Enigma between two Punjabi rappers from the MH1 channel. They were dead, sure. But were they bored? No.

Same here.

Don't get me wrong. I think giving your employees time to relax is very important. They must enjoy where they are working, otherwise you'll have to pay them a lot of money. Enjoyment is better for the company...you know why—because it's free.

And in business, free is better than paying for it. Just like in sex. Then again, in sex, sometimes when you pay for it, the quality...never mind. You must never, however, let the enjoyment get out of hand. I read about XLJ Gautam Infotech in Bangalore that took a batch of young software developers to Bangkok. One of them was found three days after his company offsite tied to the bed of a dominatrix. He resigned on the spot and didn't want to leave this dominatrix's bedroom shouting 'beat me mistress'. It's also important to know that the dominatrix was a transsexual. These things can happen. It's a standard business continuity problem. It's an act of God, like 9/11. When things like this happen it can mean one of two things—either the employee has had too much fun or someone in a cave is up to something. Usually, it's the former.

I like to call it the 'work-life balance'. I know people in HR don't use that term but I don't care—I don't have an HR department. I am my own HR. Someone suggested why I don't get my get own HR manager to find the right talent pool but I don't need any pool. I need two chairs. One for me to ask the questions and one for the candidate to answer them. In fact, at Prestige, I only had one chair for me to sit on and I interviewed Ramesh and Rashmi while they stood. Did that affect my opinion of them? Did they not sign the offer letter? That's my point.

I hate HR. What do they do that I can't do? Read resumes and talk to people? Bhola can do that. Even Antara can do that and she's not even here. Reading and talking are not skills. Cutting cost is a skill. Go to any religious place and some important person is always reading and talking—that doesn't mean he's in HR. The Pope or the main priest of the Golden Temple are not in HR. But they're qualified because of how much time they spend listening and talking to people who constantly need favours from God. You don't see them picking up resumes in their spare time from naukri.com. Anyway, you can see I have mixed feelings about this HR issue.

Point is, if you want your employees to work a 100 percent, make them work a 150 percent. But give them time off to let their hair down about 15 percent, so that when they come back they will be extra enthusiastic to make up that 15 percent and then just by momentum, deliver another 50 percent extra. Like a car that can't stop. Like Salman Khan's car. I need to work out the percentages but my logic generally works. Trust me.

And it's the new India—encourage westernification.

That means no more company picnics. That's all rubbish. Hiring a bus and going to some hill. Crap hill. If you work for Coal India and are stuck with your hideous family in Dhanbad, then go for a company picnic. Look at the view of some dam. What the fuck is the point of staring at a dam?

This is the private sector, boss. This is Mumbai. Throw away those old ideas; throw away that chutney sandwich in the tiffin box. In fact, throw away the tiffin box.

And fuck those people who go to some nonsense dinner with their parents and sit in rooms talking to the other children. These are people in their 20s, why should there be a separate children's room? In the US, people their age are all pregnant. Barack Obama is about that age—you think he spends time in the children's room at an adults' party in the White House? Twenty-year-olds should be into shots, EMIs, SMS, and Katrina Kaif.

Even though Ramesh failed, I intervened after the two calls on Friday night and said, 'I don't care who is jumping off a bridge tonight in the US, we are going clubbing!'

Now you can ask why I awarded Rashmi and Ramesh, given the fact that only she made a save. The thing is, even though I am very subtle, if I just took her while he worked, even though Ramesh may not be able to tell, he'd get a clue. That's the thing about a staff of three—if 75 percent of the people go clubbing, the remaining 25 percent can tell. Multinationals don't have that problem.

That night we went to Club Poison. I know Rizwan, who had done the club's décor. He has many businesses other than disco lights and nightclub flooring. Four that I can think of—BlackBerry repair, leather export, last minute DJ booking, and black movie tickets for Anupam Kher movies. Don't ask me why he can't come back to India. Some RAW thing. My relationship with him is that discount card he gave me on tequila in 1999 when the club opened. I still use it. That's important in business—sustainable relationships.

Remember when I was arrested? Actually, I should narrow that down. Remember when I was arrested at JFK the second time as Harun Gupta? In my interrogation, they asked me if I knew a lot of people. They asked me if I knew Osama. I told them, I have no contact with Al Qaeda but that I only deal in C-level executives (CEO, CFO), so, yes, if Al Qaeda got in touch with 1-888 about potential business collaborations, then I would meet Osama to sign the deal. I should clarify, we would be open to only phone and technology related Al Qaeda work, not terror attacks; we are not into bricks and mortar or blowing up bricks and mortar. Material costs are too high—the chemicals, explosives—besides being illegal. Even though they keep the same hours and work at night like us.

People ask me, 'Do you have no morals?' In business, never directly answer yes.

In the seventeenth century, the British East India Company sold weapons to Indians and the British to fight Indians in the same war. Revenue and profit on both sides. That's the thing about morality. You have to take sides. Not so in business. The only time you need sides in business is on the balance sheet.

And there, you have to choose the asset side over the liability side. Best way to improve your asset side is not to take sides.

But anyways, in that interrogation, Rizwan's name did come up. Some fundamentalists' guest house thing in Sanaah, Yemen. Poison Guest House. This is what I've always liked about him, never limiting his business to India. Poison nightclub here, Poison Guest House there. Patriotism in business equals bankruptcy. Some businessmen think, 'Oh, I am from this country, I should not invest elsewhere because it is my homeland' and some bullshit like that. I say, get on the plane, land wherever you land, don't sightsee and be some jackass tourist. Ask, what kind of margins can I make here? If the margins are high, stay, abandon everything in the previous place, and invest. In business, you are a citizen of profit, not nation. Rizwan knew that.

Sadly I heard they arrested him because the name 'Poison Guest House' attracted terrorists there. He didn't run a guest house saying, 'Terrorists, please come here, and make plans to poison people while I give you free breakfast'. That is the trouble with the modern world. Innocents get caught in the middle because of a word. Me. Harun. Rizwan. Poison.

When Ramesh and Rashmi walked into Poison (Mumbai nightclub), they looked like I looked when I saw a Dubai mall for the first time. In two words, shock and awe. Couldn't take in all the glamour. The point was exposure. I'm a clubber as I've explained.

London, Paris, Mumbai, I club. I don't get scared in them, even if they are throwing me out or not letting me in. They were not exposed to this. There is a simple way to get over awe. Confidence. I'm not a member of the Confederation of Indian Industry (CII) but I attend the meetings and ask questions only by virtue of confidence. I showed up four times and one guy even let me vote. In that case, a suit was important but equally important was confidence. The best way to give my employees confidence was through tequila. It worked for Tom Cruise in *Top Gun*.

And I didn't just want them to drink tequila. I wanted them to say 'tequila…'

'TEQUILA!'

'Louder, so everyone can hear it. Yeah! More shots! Waiter! Grey Goose shots…*Goose lao jaldi*! Ramesh, why is your glass empty? Why? What are you drinking? Ramesh, what are you drinking?'

'Sir, we just had the shots.'

'Fuck! What kind of answer is that man? KTF man. Keep it flowing. Where's the bar? Oh shit, it's far. Rashmi, I just want to say that you are my best call centre…person. My best. One day, you will be where I am and that day, you will take off this fuck-all salwar kameez and wear my suit.'

'Sir, I don't know how to thank you. I—excuse me. Toilet. Brfffwrghh…'

'Chicks, Ramesh. Complex.'

'Not used to booze, sir. Adjusting.'

'How?'

'By vomiting.'

'Poison is the hottest nightclub in Bombay, Ramesh. Have you never come here? Hot scene. Rocking.'

'Yes. I mean no sir. Expensive, sir.'

'What do you do Saturday nights? Sit at home and eat chips?'

'We sit as a family and watch the Baba Ramdev programme on Janmat channel and do the yoga exercises.'

'Lame. So un-American.'

'We may not go out Saturday nights sir but we are not traditional. I want to clear up that misunderstanding. We have gone to Dirty Splash Water Park in Bhandup, Inorbit Mall, we shop in Hyper-Fresh Goregaon and order from Pizza Hut every night. Plus PVR movies on Sunday. Good fun. I'm a member of Raghav's Gym and I've taken my father and sister bowling in Pleasure Lanes at Andheri. I like gelato, it is Italian. Also TGI Fridays mocktails we've had. As a family, we watch BBC, not K serials. We are new to discos only.'

'Discs...call them discs...I call it clubbing. Every weekend, I hit the clubs. This is my spot. Till I go to another spot.'

'We're learning.'

'Not bad. Not bad. I come here to check out the chicks. I wear my shades so no one recognizes me. It's cool.'

That's when they played my favourite song. Mother Fucking P.I.M.P. It's by Snoop Dogg. I wear my shades and dance to this song every time it comes on. I can't explain it. It's like a gut reaction—like standing up to the national anthem.

'Rashmi and I think you're the best, sir…just… so stylish…'

'Yes I am.'

'Please give us some tips.'

'Tell me, Ramesh, you don't look like you have a dick. Are you humping Rashmi?'

'Sir…what are you saying, sir…'

'C'mon we're just guys talking. Can you get it up? Because I want my staff to be satisfied. Are you keeping Rashmi satisfied in bed? How many times a day do you do it? Eight to nine?'

'Sir, we don't do all that.'

'So what? What about a little sex-a-holic early in the morning? I've done it at our Barista next to Prestige. Ask Bhola. Opens at seven in the morning.'

'Sir, I drink tea.'

'Fuck man. Let me touch you. Where do they make things like you? You're telling me she isn't getting any? You're both virgins! And she is still my star performer? You bastard. Do you know how many American lives she can save if you were giving it to her? What is wrong with you? If she was having it doggie style, she could probably bring people back from the dead! Idiot. How can you do this?'

'Sir, our shift is nine hours, then there's traffic. We have no flexie hours like Infocom BPO.'

'Oh man...oh man...I'm getting scared just listening to this. I'm feeling *dirtiye*...euhhh.'

'I promise I'll do all that after I have bought my family a flat in Lakhotia Hercules Malad and a Santro. It is only three months. Plus my father says sometimes you can get a rash and die.'

'Deude, in three months of marriage, I had fucked my way to Russia and not just with my wife. I was also already triple timing with *Cine Blitz* models. Don't listen to buddhas man...'

'Gautam Buddha?'

'No, not the Buddha...buddhas, buddhis...old people. With...wow, check that blonde out. Jemma Jemison...fuck-a-doodle-doo...'

'Sir, Jemma Jemison is a client?'

'Oh man...you don't watch any porn also? Why haven't you exploded yet?'

'Sir, in the office we are having some Internet issues because of ISP payment overdue. I told you about it. Plus the sites you told me about are pay by foreign credit card only. And I only have Birla Visa.'

'God help you man. Jenna Jemison is the greatest porn star in the world. *Jenna's Temptation Island*?'

'I haven't been to that island, sir.'

'It's a movie chut. Here, take this.'

'Sir, USB?'

'It's an eight hundred GB hard drive. It has nine hundred hours of porn. I carry it everywhere. I watch it everywhere. Everything. Animal, interracial, inter-galaxy, Chinese, horse, prison, historical, cartoon. Everything. It's cool. And listen carefully, first watch the videos, then try to make your own video. Watch, learn, perform, I need proof. Are you understanding me?'

'Thank you, sir.'

'If you watch this and I see that you still can't get it up, you should charge fifty rupees to show your dick to people in a circus.'

'I'm back.'

I took a second to stare at my Rashmi. Fresh look. Without the tequila haze that was there earlier. There was hope.

'You have to do something about your clothes, Rashmi. You dress like a sweeper at Heathrow airport. Here take this. Go to Millionaire boutique in Juhu and ask for Vasco. Tell him I sent you. You need tank tops. Now come, I'm taking you to the VIP area. Ramesh, stop looking at your phone. That's what people without confidence do when they cannot mingle. Or people waiting for a wire transfer from Dubai. You are neither.'

'Rashmi, your mother is getting worried, waiting for us. I just got an SMS.'

'Sshhh Ramesh. Don't talk about my mother in a nightclub no. Come…'

In front of me was a bouncer. I don't like bouncers. Especially after one night at the London Club Kali when they threw me in a dumpster. Earlier, bouncers were outside. Now they are inside. I have heard VVIP people like Mukesh Ambani have them in their bedrooms also. When 1-888 goes public (IPO), I'd like that.

'What's the problem, man in black?'

'Sir, it's a private party in here.'

'Ha. I'm one of the organizers of the private party Einstein. The chief organizer.'

'Your name?'

'Arun Goopta, the G is prominent.'

'You're not on the list, sir.'

'Are you fucking kidding me? Do you know who I am?'

'You're Arun Gupta. Sir, this is an American Consulate party. I can't let you in.'

'Listen asshole, I am the American Consulate okay.'

'No, sir, she is.'

I don't like American women from an attraction perspective. Height is the main issue. Too tall. This woman that was walking over was at least eight feet. Or six.

'I'm Susan, the Ambassador. How can I help?'

'Hello, madam. Aroon Gup–'

'Arent you the guy that just shouted at me. Jenna Jameson or something like that? Prick. Don't let him in.'

She left.

'No. It was not me. NOT ME. Eh Madam!'

This is the trouble with Americans, they never listen. The world says Pakistan, they hear Iraq. It's like that.

'Um, look, Rambo, I'm sure we can make a deal.'

'The only way I can let you into the VIP area is by champagne service.'

'Now you're talking. I don't go anywhere without champagne service. I don't wake up without drinking champagne. You think I'd sit in the VIP area without ordering champagne?'

'It's one lakh a table.'

'Okay Ramesh, Rashmi, we're just going to hang out here. On this side of the rope. The VIP area is the other side of this rope. It's pretty much the same anyway. Same floor. Same ambience. Just this side. It's cool.'

I don't remember all of this happening. Later, Ramesh and Rashmi told me what happened. I didn't believe them but I put it in this book because in any business circumstance, you should get everyone's point of view, even though you know you will finally go with yours. So that's how the offsite ended. Yes, all in all, it was a success.

Main KPIs (targets) achieved were:

1) Got Ramesh to think about his dick, which, frankly, we should all do more.
2) Got Rashmi to dress better. There is only one way you can head if you dress like a maid servant in a tea garden—upwards.
3) Both saw what Mumbai high life is.

Don't ask me how I ended up outside Hotel Bawa International in an auto rickshaw with a plate of murgh tikka and no shirt. I have absolutely no idea.

Social not working

Here's my thing on Facebook. Fine. So Mark Zuckerberg, whateverrr, 12 years old, starts Facebook and becomes a billionaire. No big deal. Okay, fine, big deal. It's a billion dollars and that doesn't come easy, unless you're Gaddafi (another hero) or Hosni Mubarak (some old Egyptian guy).

The reason I say whateverrr is that he didn't change anything. He didn't try to break the 'don't piss here' law in Singapore or protect a trillion tonnes of crops from being eaten by insects. He made people see each other's faces. Called it Facebook. Obvious. I would have called it Your Ugly Facebook because most people look like crap no matter how many side shots of their face they take with beaches behind them. It may have decreased the number of members but that would have been an authentic name.

I will have to give it to Facebook for one thing. I always thought I understood people. The way I go about it is like this—I am a person, therefore all these other people are also persons, therefore they are like me. Not exactly like me—I am a winner and they are gigantic losers—but like me because they want to do something with their lives. That is the essence of human beings. Quite like business, which involves building something with effort. Like the German man who imprisoned his own family (and himself) for twenty years or that drunk guy in Calcutta who tried to garland a Royal Bengal Tiger and was eaten. They are slightly different examples but they involved doing/building. Results.

Facebook taught me nothing. It taught me that the essence of human beings was to NOT build. To do nothing. To sit at home all day and throw birds and sheep at each other online. And give each other updates of their minute-by-minute boring uneventful fuck-all lives till everyone is swimming in an interconnected circuit of six hundred million middle-class banal updates.

The worst effect it has is on teenagers who grow up with no real life values—they don't know what it is like to skip school and watch *Disco Dancer* (westernified Bollywood film), they don't know what it's like stealing money from parents and buying cigarettes, or getting caught by Govind's dad while humping in an old abandoned warehouse (sorry Rajshree, Govind promised the factory was closed. By the way, great news on the UNDP posting).

I hope I have presented to you both sides of a balanced mature debate on Facebook. Now, moving on to Rashmi. I told Ramesh to check out Rashmi's Facebook page. I was going to ask Rashmi to do the same for Ramesh. Later. At this point, I see more potential in her than him mainly because she is a go-getter and he is an idiot. I am interested in her Facebook because I am interested in her person. Anyone I see potential in, I want to know more. And by more I mean everything. Ramesh has no potential right now, so like him, his Facebook will be boring, just his stupid face and no one looking at it. So best to use him now with his best qualities which is running servant-like errands and obeying things I say. She, however, could have other things going on in her life that need to be monitored in case it gets in the way of her life with me. In the office, anyone who says you shouldn't have favourites has never worked in an office. Anyway, here is the email he sent:

Dear Sir,

Following are the contents on Rashmi's site. Please note and provide feedback. The needful will be done.

Ramesh.

On entry, through the stolen password, I immediately noticed the 'friends' number. Low, sir. Twenty-five. Mostly former colleagues at Hanes and other BPOs. Prominent is one Varsha. She has the most entries on her wall, the most recent being 'sup girl'. Maybe she meant soup, sir.

Good. Twenty-five is not a lot of friends. It means she isn't one of those types spending hours on Facebook filling out surveys on whether she has an artistic mind or what movies say about the shape of her legs or whatever. To clarify, that's what people tell me. I have not done one of these surveys. And I have to thwack Ramesh next time I see him. How can he not know that 'sup' means 'what's up' and not soup? Fucking fool.

Sir, she has joined two fan clubs—'SRK forever' and 'Star World Fan Club'. The first one is set up by Malaysian fans dedicated to Shah Rukh Khan sir and his daily movements, and the Star World one is just a list of the day's programmes. It is run by a young Chinese person, Ms Lili Yip, marketing manager, Star TV, out of Hong Kong.

I don't have an issue with Shah Rukh Khan. Why? Most of his fan base is in Germany, Switzerland, or New Jersey. In fact, if you ask people in India, most people think he is a cricketer (because he spends more time waving from stadiums than he does making movies). That's why no issues. Like me, he looks West for his paying audience. And Star World programming is always good. That's how I know when to watch Oprah Winfrey's show. Yesterday's was 'Seven Things for the Best Pregnancy Ever'. I really got into it. Maybe Rashmi and I can watch it together.

Oh, sir, I also noticed she is friends with that Ann Sipkins at New York St John's Archdiocese. The Madam Anne who taught us, sir. She has left a comment on the wall:

Thanks for the message, Rashmi. Next time I'm looking for rosaries I'll be sure to look up www.outsourcedcatholicstuff.com. I had no idea it was run from Mumbai. I'm glad you asked but no sodomy does not involve any board games—that's monopoly. I will love to discuss this more but I have members of my seminary on this page, so why don't you write me an email and I'll explain it.

And also that Brad. The Homo. He is on here also. I didn't know his name was Brad Hard. I went to his page, sir. His photo is a poster of some show. It says Stand-up Comedy. He's a bit like Navjot Sidhu, sir, this Brad Hard, but he seems to be dressed as a banana. The show is called Hard On—Uncensored. It is at the Greenwich Street Theatre from September 3 to September 7 at 8 pm, interchanging with Waiting for Godot by Samuel Beckett. I am just giving the information as I am seeing on the page.

Very nice. Staying in touch with her teachers. If I hadn't started that fire after the ISC finals and shot chemistry Banerjee's dog, Hastings, maybe I could have been in touch with some of my teachers as well. About Brad Hard. This new play seems better than the last one.

Sir, Rashmi has linked a Baba Ramdev YouTube video. He is giving stock market tips while doing yoga. Eight hundred people have liked this post, sir. Including you. It looks like 430 thumbs ups came from you sir between 2:41 and 3:33 am last Saturday night.

First, that's wrong, I'm not on Facebook. Second, on Saturdays I club, you all know that by now. Third, I know he is not Westernified but I need to learn about leadership from Baba. Multitasking. And billions of Indians love him. He is onto something. I'm seeing him everywhere. The other day, there was a poster of him at Big Bazaar.

Sir, Rashmi has also taken the survey, 'Is Justin Timberlake hot?'

She didn't need to do that. I could have told her. Yes. But I am glad she is doing a survey of Justin Timberlake. I would be pissed if she had taken a Dino Morea survey. You don't know who that is? Neither do I. Just a name I saw on a hoarding for a shit movie called 'Blood Factory' and thought, most Dinos I know repair VCD players.

So from this, I had no cause of alarm or concern about Rashmi. She was what she was, which is rare in business. You don't know how many times you will open a shipment and the thing you signed the consignment for is not there, and something else is there, even a person maybe. Not so with Rashmi. As Facebook tells me, if you ordered Rashmi and presented the bill of lading, you would get Rashmi. She is transparent like that. See-through.

In business, transformation is everything. There is a very famous proverb in wildlife—You can take a horse to the water but you cannot make it drink. It's a stupid proverb. This is why wildlife people live in the wild without a haircut. It's your damn horse, why can't you make it drink? That's what I say.

Ramesh and Rashmi aren't horses. I know that. Also, as I explained earlier, there's plenty of water in the Prestige Business Centre. What I am referring to is an analogy (foreign people reading this will understand that). The point is, once you've made the horse drink, can you also transform it into a faster animal—maybe a cheetah? That's where real business skills lie. Like the guy heading Emirates Airlines who transformed it from some crap Middle-Eastern carry-people-on-donkeys service to the world's largest airline. This person understood transformation. He understood that to change, first you had to stop carrying people on donkeys and buy airplanes. Besides, there is no way you can get to London on a donkey in five hours from Dubai. That's a basic business understanding. It's the same with Rashmi.

Nowadays, people have this thing called a blog. Honestly, blog equals shit. A blog is a place where everyone is a writer. Now, here's my thing. If everyone is a writer, why the fuck am I writing a memoir? Why don't I blog it? The answer is simple—do you see blogs at Crossword? No, you see books. The biggest problem with blogs is that publishers haven't been able to think of how to bind it properly or what kind of a cover to give it. Till those things are sorted, no one will buy blogs. Till then, I'll be writing books. And besides, most blogs are on the Internet, which means two minutes into reading someone has another screen up and is masturbating. You can't do that with a book. You can't be reading the Google story and playing with your dick. It doesn't happen that way.

In any business, setting up the infrastructure is everything. You wouldn't start a bakery without an oven. It's like that with publishing blogs. And bloggers—that's the industry term—are not mainly writers. They essentially cut and paste from other bloggers. See, I don't do that. I write down things. Sometimes I ask Bhola (I sent him to Harish Basic Computer Skills) to cut and paste some things—facts—but that's not writing. That's Bhola. But with bloggers, what I do they replace with what Bhola does. So if I was a blogger, I would be Bhola, which I don't want to be because they just burnt down his house in Jharkhand over some land dispute. We're digressing from the main point. The point here is Rashmi.

I told Rashmi to keep a blog of her transformation. Without westernification, she is nothing, always chasing China. She was a good learner, she understood that. A blog would track this westernification. Going from maid servant to CEO is a bigger change than IBM going from a computer-making company to a consulting company. Why did I do that when I personally hate blogs? Simple. Rashmi is not a writer, nor are bloggers, so A intersection B, if you know your math. Besides, I needed to keep an eye on the changes without actually showing up at her house every day (I had thought about that). If you were in the perishables business, you would do a spot check on your inventory to see if it wasn't rotten. This is not exactly like that but still. The main thing is that I wanted to check on her changes without checking. Step by step to see tangible growth. Like salesforce.com. Updating sales opportunities is the employee's responsibility but anytime you need to see sales performance, just log in and take a data extraction. If there are no sales, you know what to do.

Here it's slightly different because you can't record individual activities leading to westernification. It's a much more gradual process, like making an iPhone out of a semi-conductor chip (minus beating up a Chinese worker). Westernification is mental and physical. It doesn't just happen by buying Metro heels and a Triumph bra and some Revlon lipstick. It's from the inside. Like the way *Newsweek* was transformed by firing everyone.

It was not important to me what Rashmi was wearing (obviously, sleeveless is better, everyone is into that over there), but what she was thinking was what mattered. Real transformation starts in the mind. Was she having enjoyable sexual thoughts? Was she telling her mother, 'Paratha—whatever, Dirty Splash Water World—yes'? That shows in her—like one of my heroes, Ramalingam Raju—resolve. In his case, never deviating from defrauding. In her case, confidence. People often ask me, 'Arun, why don't we have an Indira Gandhi in London and New York? Why doesn't Indira Gandhi cross over like our crossover movies, like *Slumdog*?' The answer is confidence. If Indira Gandhi was told to eat parathas and asked why she was home late, would she order the army to shoot everyone? That's what stands between Rashmi and Meghan. An army. Of confidence.

I will quote directly from Rashmi's blog. She thought I didn't know it's her blog because she wrote it as MumbaiWackyGurrl, but Ramesh told me it's hers. Also, I can tell from the words she uses because sometimes I use the same words. That's my intuition, and it's critical in business. Only on intuition did my hero Donald Trump decide that New York will be a good place for skyscrapers. Before him, there was nothing there. Desert. It's my Donald Trump intuition that made me follow MumbaiWackyGurrl and, like his skyscrapers, I saw her rise.

I mentioned to Ramesh that I will quote her and he said it might be plagiarism. Whoever thinks so, come and see me and I'll fuck you up. This is not plagiarism. When yoga teachers quote directly from the Gita, you don't have a problem. When Supreme Court judges quote from the constitution, you don't disturb them. Then leave me alone.

> January 17
>
> Fought with mama today over the pole. Refused to eat her paratha for the first time but it's not my fault. KFC's Golden Shower card is expiring and I never get

to go. And she doesn't like fried chicken even though it's in Khar and I love it. I don't want to be like those Ekta Kapoor daughters but sometimes I want things and she wants different things for me and I need to tell her. Arun sir and Anne madam also said about being assertive.

I agree. If you want fried chicken legs, don't let your mother get in the way. Old India will always try to stop you but nothing should come between New India and its chicken. Ask Mahendra Singh Dhoni. I am sure he has a KFC gold card.

February 14

Went with Ramesh to Dirty Splash. Arun sir's discount coupons were valid from 2012 and this was only 2010. Still, they gave us a discount and Ramesh was handed a condom. He got nervous and started giggling. I don't think they get a lot of people during the day and the people that come, usually come for all that. I saw a lot of older office type men with young women and the women called the men sir. I asked Ramesh maybe they are secretaries and these are office people having affairs but he said that only happens in 3-star hotels. Naturally with swimming costumes and all, this would be a good place to escape your wife and say you are on some business trip. Ramesh couldn't understand. Sometimes, I think he is too childish. He was nervous because he had never worn a swimming costume in front of a girl and I had never worn that in front of a colleague. Varsha (a girl I worked with at Hanes

Underwear Returns) and I had gone rain dancing for the quarter-end party when we were at 24/7 call centre but we had got wet, not total swimming costume like this. When we were coming down the Pagal Rakshash Triple Water Slide, Ramesh was holding me and I was holding him. It was nice.

Not like that time when Vishal (Hanes Call Centre) had tried to kiss me when I went to him with that customer problem. I didn't like that. Also because he said he loved me but had only joined as Helpdesk Manager that morning. I know the tricks of most men. After the Hanes shifts, all day fixing British people's underwear fitting problems, when I tried to sleep in the Scorpio, Harminder would try to touch my... Anyway, it's nice to work for a call centre with only one other person. It's different. Also, Ramesh is scared and especially scared of me. Quite cute. Like Ritesh Deshmukh, but handsome. We were both in swimming costumes, falling, shouting, water was under us. It was nice. We spent four hours there and when Ramesh went to buy us some gelato, I felt one creepy fellow looking at me. I quickly went and changed.

That was me behind them. I wasn't creepy, I was dressed as Kapil Dev. I was incognito.

March 23

Went to Millionaire boutique as sir asked me to. Met Vasco. When I told him about Arun sir and the discount, he told me there was no discount. Later, I went with Varsha and just shopped normally. I had never bought a suit before and that too, Pantaloon. I've seen photos of Ms Naina Lal Kidwai and Ms Shikha Sharma who are important business women in India and they wear saris. Maybe because they look at Indian businesses. Arun sir says, if you want to do business with the West, you must look at the West and look like the West. I agree.

Obviously she either went to the wrong Millionaire or met the wrong Vasco. Vasco and I have been friends for years. Ever since I helped him in that spurious vodka case in Gandhinagar. He would never deny me clothes.

March 29

Okay, yes, last night at Hard Rock Café in Worli, I told Ramesh to kiss me. I know he wanted to. He kept talking about some IIPM MBA cut-off he missed. It's not that I've never been kissed, it's just that it's a nice thing. And he's a nice guy. I didn't know he was saving money to get an ICICI loan for his family. Anyway, two shots and I was gone and I was leaning on his shoulder but he kept talking about home loans or some crap. He hadn't seen any Karan Johar movies or what? That's the time to kiss Kajol. I'm not Kajol but still, as a guy, he should. If this was college...anyway, about thirty minutes later, when he kissed me, the waiters started dancing on the table. I thought it was because of us but apparently they do it every half an hour. The song was YMCA and I know it from MTV. Cyrus Broacha did some dance to it. I had never seen a restaurant where waiters dance on tables—if you did this at Mocha, they would throw you out. I know because Varsha did it after her board results.

This movie that sir had given Ramesh, he was telling me what all is in there. My god. I mean, I am open-minded but my god. And then he asked me if I want to try them. I slapped him and left. I didn't even know how far the Worli station was.

You know what this is? This is her taking charge of her own sex life. Like when the founder of Google came back as CEO. This is like that, but for virgins. Donald Trump says virgins are less productive as managers than well-sexed people. I couldn't agree more. I'm helping you Roshomon.

April 3

Varsha said at CCD today, 'How can you do suicides ya? Dead bodies. People are dying. I would cry.' Thing is, I don't think like that. I think like Arun sir says. Everything is a business. When I was working for Hanes underwear, without underwear, it was also a life and death situation no? When someone is stuck in a highway in a storm...that is a life and death situation no? So this is like that. Only slightly more pressure because it is actual. I remember when I was doing LG washing machine returns, a lady told me that, without her washing machine for more than three days, she would die. She had four children in school. Here, without my help, someone would really die. And when I got 4 LG SuperMaxx washer-dryers working, my boss gave me four points and a new Nokia phone. Here, if I save four lives, same thing. Outsourcing is outsourcing, that's what Arun sir says. Varsha got some job in Dubai. Double fixed pay. I am not jealous. Five more lives and I will ask for an increment.

Excellent explanation. Yes, life and death are no big deal as long as you can put them on a board and put numbers next to it.

April 7

I saw the video sir had given Ramesh. I cannot write down anything about it. I will just say this. I took a long shower. Most nights, we have no water in the building. This night, it was there. Arun sir is right, everything happens for a reason. He was talking about the crash on Wall Street but I was talking about…I am not going to write this down.

No comment. One comment. Yes. It's happening. If you don't know what I mean, four words—Sharon Stone, *Basic Instinct* (comma is not a word).

April 7

Ramesh called again. He knows mama goes out to give tuition and I am sleeping. And it's only been forty minutes since I saw him. And again, he's talking about all that. Yes baba, I saw the video. No, I didn't close my eyes, I'm not some baby okay. Yeah I know how to do some of those things. Mama's school sports day is tomorrow. Arun sir is in the US. I said he can come here. He got damn excited. I'll be honest, I think I did too. Shit, I will delete this post soon.

Must find out everything. That's the problem with blogs. They stop at the critical moment. This does not happen with sextube.com.

April 8

If you go to Shoppers Stop early in the morning, seven o' clock, they don't open. But there is this girl from the Northeast, June, I've made friends with her. She does my make-up for free. The make-up there is so much nicer. Foreign brands—Revlon and all (from what I use, the stuff I bought in the Mumbai local trains, I once got pimples). June doesn't ask for money but has only one request—she doesn't like to take the train home alone so sometimes she asks me to go home with her. She's in Goregaon (east). I don't mind. When she takes the train alone, because she is from there, Arunachal, people eve tease her. Sometimes, they whistle but also touch. I have to say it's never happened to me. This one guy once said, 'Chh chh', but I slapped him and two ladies pushed him off at Matunga. June and her mother moved from Delhi because in her college they tried to grab her during some fest. So her mother, Dina aunty runs Excelsior Salon in Goregaon east. She said Arshad Warsi and Navjot Sidhu have both gone there for waxing but I don't believe it. She told me to come for a full body waxing but I am scared of how much it will hurt (I've never done back and legs, I shave). They have some new thing called laser. Arun sir and we were watching this movie *Dirty Dancing* (his second favourite film) and Arun sir said the best thing he liked about the movie was how everyone was waxed. Especially the hero, Patrick Swayze. US people apparently wax every week. I am too scared (hurts a lot) but I will go to her because she will do it for free she said.

That Ramesh is so naughty, I told him about getting myself waxed and he sent me some Carmen Electra link on bikini waxing. Naughty. I'm not into all that but over there, in the US, those women are into anything, no limits on the body. It is smooth though.

Grooming is everything. I wax my whole body. Without waxing, I would never get equity funding.

April 9

Ramesh bought me some earrings and Chetan Bhagat's *Two States of My Marriage*. I don't like the earrings, they're too long and too behnji but I didn't tell him. If I wear them, I will look like some Bhojpuri actress. I wish he'd got me something from Shoppers Stop. Anyway, it's sweet, especially because he also has that family home loan. The brochure of his building, Lakhotia Hercules, looks sexy and modern—stilt parking and almost 12 hours non-stop water. I wanted the book because I hadn't read it. Chetan Bhagat is hot.

Yes he is.. Another hero of mine.

A date

Dating is a nonsensical American thing. It's like arranged marriage but arranged by the couple themselves. Double the amount of work. Half the pleasure because the humping is on an 'evaluate and decide' mode. It's like a Bridge Loan with a recall facility.

But when Ramesh and Rashmi suggested that I date, I didn't say no. In business, always be open to listening. Imagine what would happen if you ignored the sentence 'your CEO is dead' or 'there is no oil left'. Therefore, always be open to anything. That's how ONGC now owns oil fields in Ukraine.

Thing is, I wasn't lonely when Antara left. No no. Earlier, during Cleopatra's time and even in the 1960s, there were huge problems when a wife left because cooking was mostly on gas cylinders and she had the monopoly market by knowing how to cook. Like Barclays in the UK with savings accounts in the 1980s. If you wanted to open one, you had to go to them. Wives and being fed is similar. But nowadays, there are take-out menus, *Masterchef,* which has my hero Akshay

Kumar, teaching me quick things to do to babycorn while shouting at a housewife from Ranchi, websites, burrp.com—I can never spell it correctly in Google, and always end up at a Bulgarian porn site—but the point is that now there are many options.

Also, I had the double advantage of Bhola. It was an August morning when she announced she's leaving. I remember because it was raining nationwide and another Air India plane crashed into a Coimbatore zoo because the pilot was snoozing After an hour of what I viewed as conversation and she as argument, Bhola was being pulled on either side by Antara and me. I was about to tell her that I had almost saved enough for that Burberry replacement she wanted (I made a mistake in Dubai and bought Burberrie. No one told me the right spelling, so how would I know that it was a fake?), when at 11:43 am and 12 seconds, she said, 'Enough'. That's not why I remember so much of that day. No, I remember that day because, while we were windswept and tugging at our cook in the pouring rain, I knew I'd get to have Bhola's alu-gobi-mattar forever, and she wouldn't. This was because he was leaning, yes, in my direction. Now you may say you had an unfair advantage Arun because you had three people pulling with you. I can say, why didn't she think of that? Why didn't she bribe three loitering auto-drivers to say, 'Eh, thoda help karo?'

And I didn't just pull Bhola in my direction, Bhola pushed himself in my direction, psychologically.

He wanted to be with me. Perhaps knowing that I had hidden his Pan card without which most of his adult life's aspirations in India were useless. We both knew Bhola made another spectacular thing, which I thought was chilli chicken but was corrected and told, 'Sir, chettinad' from (he claimed) Kerala.

I knew chettinad is from Chennai (in fact, it's Chennai's Tamil name) but sometimes you have to not correct illiterates. Like children, you have to let it go. So that when push comes to pull and there you are in the middle of a terrible monsoon day, in the parking area of Raheja Corleone Versova west, holding on to your cook while letting go of your wife, he knows which direction to take.

The payoff—three years later, there's a woman coming over and you have the cook advantage. Whatever the future had in store for us after that tug-o-cook, I ate it. And now, this thing, I mean person, would enjoy the culinary benefits. Okay, who is this person? Like I said, it's a woman. No, not VC Sarah. I would never get Bhola to go to the market for that, she could accuse me of wasting 1-888 money on broccoli. No, this was...well don't be curious, this is not *Stardust*. Just because I'm writing a book doesn't mean I have to share. That New York Governor, Eliot Spitzer wrote a memoir—he didn't mention he was buying whores. No, I'm not buying whores but... look, point is, a man, a visionary, sometimes gets lonely. That's why Vijay Mallya has a yacht. With the Internet, loneliness is reduced.

I'm not doing this because Rashmi and Ramesh told me about secondshaadi.com. I am not into being coaxed. I am the coaxer. Yes, perhaps there was some coaxing. Rashmi had said, 'Sir, you must try it. My uncle met the same wife he was married to and now they are happy again.' So yes, the coaxer can become the coaxee, the jailer in jail, it's a common syndrome. The thing is, this is a fellow entrepreneur, a millionaire, shaadi.com's guy who's launched secondshaadi.com, so I went to the website to support it. Like the CEO of JP Morgan going to the CEO of Goldman's son's birthday party. Or people wearing flag pins on Republic Day. This is exactly that.

Brilliant idea by the way, you already have a customer base of a million on shaadi.com. Just constantly message them every day and tell them to leave their disgusting spouse and suddenly you get a spike in subscribers to the new site. I do hear that shaadi.com's biggest subscribers are uncles, aunts, touts, fixers—the lifeblood of India's arranged marriage engine. In which case, you're fucked. No point emailing some fixer uncle in New Jersey asking if your husband beats you. No emotional connect there. Antara and I met in the Delhi Hyatt coffee shop and fell in love by the way. No arranged anything. Except Romesh uncle. I had no idea he was a broker till I saw papa's pass book years later. Point is, we both ordered spaghetti bolognese and it began. You didn't need a yearly subscription of Rs 3,500 with auto renewal to marry back then. Thank you, Indira Gandhi.

So who cares if I met Tina on secondshaadi.com where I was Raghav, a 22 year old from Princeton? And does it really matter that when she asked me if I was a fan of the Medieval Pundits, I told her I am an atheist? I'm not into music so how would I know? Musicians should really not name themselves after priests, it confuses everyone. I would not listen to a band called The Upanishads. It would confuse people. Like having another company called Citibank that home delivers Mexican food. Two conflicting brands throw off consumers. Musicians are shit people, always confusing us with their names. Except Michael Bolton, he's very good.

Okay, yes, there was another knowledge gap. On G-chat, she asked if I thought the actor Shahid Kapur was cute. And I said yes, and described all the credentials of his father Pankaj Kapur. But recovery is everything in business (just ask the bankrupt people at Palm Inc—who uses a palm pilot?), so I immediately said that they should push him higher up the batting order. Now, I can't help it if she had no idea who Shahid Afridi was. A proper negotiation takes two honest parties. Otherwise you have an abandoned merger like Bharti Telecom in Africa.

Ramesh's Wikipedia link came too late. Several things here. It's not my fault that she doesn't know Karamchand, only India's greatest TV detective. Second, not knowing this does not portray me as an old person as I overheard Rashmi telling Ramesh on her tapped phone. My son Henry knows about

Mohenjo-daro. Does that mean he lived in a hut there in 4000 BC?

I should also clarify. Why Henry? I named him after Ford. I don't care if Antara changed it to Gaurav, the man who discovered the assembly line deserves to have a child named after him. I wanted him to go to Doon School where it would help. Henry has a much better chance of being admitted than Gaurav. In business, always know your customer's background. Whoever he is, become that. Everyone at Doon has English names. Don't stick out with Gaurav. Don't buy into the argument that diverse names help. When companies say you help diversity, it means you're not getting promoted. You're getting a cookie in a plastic plate by some fat HR lady saying diversity is good while non-diverse people go home in their Ferraris. As King Lear once said, 'To belong, you have to belong' (It could also have been the Bihar Chief Minister Nitish Kumar talking to rediff.com. I didn't get time to check).

Age is not given away by Pankaj Kapur. Age is given away by how I G-chatted with this woman, which in a word was—suavely. I knew all the latest phrases like 'LOL' and 'GET OUT OF HERE' and 'FUCK YOU' (that backfired) and 'NO WAY. ROTFLMAO'. Sometimes content is less important than confidence. Earlier, I had mentioned this in reference to nightclubs. How you dress, what you say, and how you carry yourself. Did Richard Branson know anything about the airline business when he got into it from Virgin Records? But he learnt the important phrases like 'passenger' and 'boarding' and 'ticket counter' and that got him through. I sent a copy of my G-chat conversation to Ramesh and Rashmi for their thoughts on it. Even they had no idea what I was talking about. That's how young and trendy I was.

An important lesson about romance—exchange of knowledge in romance is useless. It's not like business where information is power. Here, lack of information is power. She knows less and she wants to meet me. This does not happen in the newspaper business. If you found three blank areas in the *Economic Times*, you would not want to sleep with the editor to get the three missing articles. Every field is different. This is known as target marketing.

So I displayed limited knowledge of young people's habits. What was the result? She came to see me didn't she? And Bhola made a candlelight dinner didn't he? (Almost better because the electricity bill...never mind). So the Internet worked. Always listen to Bill Gates.

I left the door a little open. That shows expectation but not over-enthusiasm.

'Um. I'm looking for Raghav. Are you Raghav's dad?'

Her perfume was very strong. Reminded me of Emirates business class and its bathroom that I often use (And fuck you air hostess Irene Ward if you are reading this. There is no sign that says economy class passengers can't use it. It's the same plane).

'I'm Raghav.'

The other thing I noticed were the boobs. Huge. I think young women nowadays take the same steroids that Olympic 100 metre sprinters take. And she was wearing something corset-like that pushed them up. I could understand that. When Hewlitt Packard's printer sales were down, they pushed up the PC division. Same thing. Highlight what's working.

Also it struck me that this person was twenty-seven years younger. And when we married and if I died and she took over the empire, possibly ten billion by then, Ramesh and Rashmi would be older than her and it would be tough for them to take orders from her. Also by then, they would understand business cycles much better than someone who only has boobs to work with. That's the other thing about building an empire—always marry well. And marry her looks and management potential before you marry her. Imagine a board meeting where she is wearing this corset. And imagine Mukesh Ambani or Warren Buffet are on the board (which they will be soon). How would it look? I immediately knew this was not going to work because of a possible management stalemate in fifteen years. It happened at Newscorp when Rupert Murdoch married a younger Chinese woman. She spoke at the News Corp board meeting and his children, all senior managers, couldn't understand the language. Yes, in business, knowing a foreign language is important but not to this extent.

'You don't look like anything in the picture.'

'Neither do you.'

She didn't. In the picture, she had a yellow bag. Now she had no bag. People lie so much in photos.

Granted it was the wrong time for the jamadar to come and abuse me about unpaid bills but you can't plan everything. Who knew about the Japanese earthquakes or Libya's revolution? Anyways, she didn't need to see that fight. Maybe she didn't notice. She had enough time to drink water and take in my luxurious accommodation (Prajakat Housing Society is not for everyone. Exclusive. Even the builder advertized it as, '*Not* for the who's who').

Once I showered and put mercurochrome to heal my wound, we resumed.

'You are not 22.'

'Time flies.'

This was true. We hadn't emailed each other in five days.

'Madam, dinner.' Bhola served her the broccoli cheese pasta that I had seen Akshay Kumar making in his show. Now it's good that she turned and left. In business we call that a fortunate outcome without investment. Subhomoi Sen, State Bank of India manager explained this to me in his own words, 'Mr Gupta, you see, before the world financial crisis in 2007, everyone was investing, growing, acquiring. We did nothing. And look, today we came out losing nothing. That's why we can't give you a loan for your suicide.'

I hate Subhomoi Sen but this is like that. I did not invest but got the desired result. Yes, Rashmi and Ramesh were eager to know the next day what had happened. The concern is nice. It shows the kind of team I've built—dedicated in work, life, death, and love. I said, 'There's no time for love in outsourcing.' I wasn't lying. Do you think Warren Buffet will take his eyes off his billions in portfolios across the world to have a date at home with cheese and broccoli with a lady who works for Mudra spending all day adjusting the font in R-ADAG and her evening pushing her boobs up on secondshaadi.com? What happens if, in that time, the Nikkei crashes or the US Treasury dips?

Would it have been nice to be invited to NASSCOM and go with someone perfuming up the entire ITC ballroom? Yes. When the IPO happens, would it be nice to be on the NASDAQ balcony with someone other than Bhola in case Ramesh and Rashmi's visas are denied, which they most likely will be? Maybe. But those are cosmetic. Like Mahindra adding 'rise' to their corporate logo. Ultimately, no matter who rose, they will be judged by their trucks. I will thus be judged by American lives, not Mudra boob love.

That's the conclusion on this love venture—no go.

Managing crisis. When Rome burnt, we did not.

That dating experience made me realize three things. First, once I came back to the market, the love market, I was a perfect catch. Second, girls like Tina lie on websites. Third, why do I need to pay shaadi.com commission+ISD rates? Maybe down the line, once I have saved one of my own callers, conversation can turn from trauma to chat to why don't you come to Mumbai and let's marry?

They say don't date at work but fuck them. They don't work 24/7/365. The only way I wouldn't date at work is if I could extend the number of days in a year. Which, right now, is a bit hard.

I'll always remember September 19, 2008. I like to refer to it as our 9/11/26/7/7. I saved a seven there but you know what I mean—I merged the two tragedies of London 7/7 and Mumbai 26/7. You always have to do that in business—merge and make things redundant. The other seven was redundant, just like Atari was once Nintendo came out with Game Box.

'Sir, there's an unusually high number of calls today,' Rashmi said, and returned to her damaged headset. And that was 6 am.

Look, I am updated with world events so I knew that Lehman Brothers had declared bankruptcy the day before. They, and other Wall Street people, were involved in starting a financial crisis that eventually made all Americans homeless and the country of Iceland had to be sold. But that would be months later. Today, from 6 am, I couldn't tell what was going on. Essentially it had to do with home mortgages. They took people's mortgages and sold it to other people. Sometimes, they sold it to the same people.

It's an important lesson in business. Reading the fine print. Looking at what you're buying. You already have a mortgage. Why are they selling you your mortgage? Who allowed them? Why did you not keep your mortgage more carefully under lock and key? And did it not strike you, you fool, that you are buying the same thing twice? That's why I am not in favour of illiterate people going into business. I read an article about how post-Communism or whatever, Russian mafia bosses became billionaires but they couldn't read or write. Look at them today, all in jail. That's the thing—if you can't read print, then you'd have a tough time with the fine print, which is a thinner version of that and even harder.

I should take a step back here and explain to my non-business readers two things. One, you should not be reading this, this is a business memoir and second, lots of people say that Wall Street is not just a term. Wall Street is an idea. What Wall Street does is spread across the world. That's nonsense. It is a real street in downtown Manhattan and whatever happens there is all that happens. They have a bull on that street. Made of iron. That's the bull of the bull and the bears. At the other end, they have a bear. I think it's real but some say it's made of iron also. Point is, between the bull and the bear, on this street is Wall Street. So if any fool—and lots of fools say this—comes up to you and says, 'I work on Wall Street', and if he doesn't actually work between the bull and the bear, don't listen to him.

Normally, we got about a hundred calls a night, which meant that we could talk to each customer calmly and have a whole three minutes to save each of them. Some people may think three minutes is too short when someone has to pour out their deepest insecurities, but it isn't. Not if you tell them to hurry up. Okay yes, that's only five hours on the phone when we work twelve-hour shifts but it's not like the rest of the time we fuck around. This is not some school where I encourage dirty SMS chats between teenagers in some canteen. Actually, I encourage dirty SMSes, but that's a different thing for a different productivity reason. Notable thing here is, the Prestige Business Centre has no canteen. In fact, there's nothing to eat or drink. No, I'm not a madman. There's water. Sometimes, I substitute it with Red Bull but they can't tell that except that one time when Ramesh said,

'Sir, this is Red Bull.' Closest dinner is KFC and that's ten minutes. If you are in battle, say in Faullujah, can you stop and say, wait, I need to have a masala chai and a dahi vada? That's what I keep telling Ramesh and Rashmi.

This is like that. When an American is dying, can you tell him, 'Sir, I understand your entire savings base is wiped out but I really want a Chicken McNugget right now'? That's what I don't understand about IBM and Accenture and all those Bangalore call centres with those Café Coffee Days and McDosas and 20 year old men tugging 20 year old women's salwar kameez's. What's the point of those massive cafeterias? Are you in the outsourcing business or the catering business? And it adds up. Coffee plus dosa plus water coolers plus frankies plus Coke fountains, and very soon you can't tell the difference if this is a multinational or a PVR.

Anyway, returning to our Modi Operandi, I make my employees spend the rest of the time learning. Watching US TV shows (Bhola gets original pirated ones), looking up suicide statistics across different states to see which is rising (account planning—always critical), latest Hollywood films on YouTube, reading leading US publications like *People* magazine, *TV Guide*, and *USA Today*. On Facebook I insisted that they make only US friends, especially if they don't know them. Sure, most of the people respond with rejections and 'I don't know you' but see what's happening here—there's direct communication with

Americans and a direct chance of reading how they write. On Twitter, same thing, easy to do, follow only by location. Everyday, they have a goal of following a hundred US people. It's not a big task. That way, in 130 characters, they get an every second update on US language. I was tempted to start a Twitter quiz and randomly ask, 'What did @camerondiaz say?' but I know these two. They are diligent. They would respond with 'Mascara's running. LA's hot. Down with Wall Street greed. Love you fans. 12:21 pm, Sept 19' and right there, they've heard a US person. Also, nobody knows this (nobody asks, this is a shit country when it comes to curiosity), but I also send them out to eavesdrop on conversations of American tourists in Colaba. It's a hit-and-miss because a lot of our tourists are fuckers from Spain and France and UK, so they may be diluted by some other rubbish accent but I tell them to tune into the US one.

See the thing is, learning is everything in business. Without learning, Swami Vivekananda would just be a guy in an orange turban looking for an auditorium in Chicago. Nobody would have named important intersections in Pune after him. Without learning, the stock market would just look like a bunch of numbers going up and down. Once you learn, you would know that they are a bunch of numbers going up and down. Bhola often asks, 'Sir, you are so knowledgeable about the US, why didn't you do an MBA? You are the ideal candidate.' I'll reveal here, now, that Harvard Business School asked. And that I thought about it. In fact, most of the time the applicant has to write an essay but in this case, they wrote me an essay. See, the thing is, I know Boston (that's where HUBS is, HUBS being the abbreviation insiders use) and I wouldn't go there just as a student like they wanted me to. I would go as a partner.

I really see that as the next step in the Executive MBA programs. Anyone can pay or get a loan or a scholarship to sit in a class but if a business school believes in you, they want you because you are a twenty-first century business visionary (I mean me), they should let you teach. Many reasons for this—they've ruined your weekend clubbing plans by making you sit in a room listening to some Amartya Sen type deude who will take your entire three year course term to finish one sentence. They've ruined your dinner plans for desi potluck. Least they can do is let you teach Basics of Marketing so you can hit on young white chicks. I'm not a pervert. I am a truthteller. That's why I proposed this to the dean when he came to speak at the India Today Conclave in Delhi and I cornered him in the urinal till he gave me his email. (By the way, you would think that the dean of Harvard has a big but…never mind). Was I aggressive? Yes, a little bit. But you have to be. It's called beating a drum. Yours. Do you think people would know Pepsico if they just put out one small ad in the Indian Express classifieds? That's how I emailed him my proposal and that's why I got the essay back. Later, my lawyer said it was a Cease and Desist letter but these Americans have many terms for many things. Even though it's my business to know American lingo and spread it, sometimes I'm behind. In summary, I rejected HUBS.

Look, would I like to take calls all twelve hours? Sure. More calls, more lives, more money...who wouldn't? But you don't have to pay the international dialling rates, I do. And international dialling rates versus suicidee per second, if you do the graph and project the numbers (I made Ramesh do it), you will find that optimum revenue per caller is reached at three minutes. Anything more or less and your costs outweigh letting them live. I'd make a lot more money if my phone bills were subsidized but neither those Florida bastards nor VC Sarah reimburses me. So I tell Rashmi and Ramesh to keep the calls tight. Keep it concise and valuable. Whoever can't be saved in three minutes is not worth saving. The STD bill outweighs their life. Simple math, as they say at HUBS.

We worked almost seven hours straight on September 19. I got fucked with the bills later but it was net net net lucrative. Now, at an average, among customers, we get a lot of actors. I can understand that. No money, no roles, all actors are waiters in the US (yes even Brad Pitt). This is what people don't know. See the thing is, they have so much time between movies that they are often bored of watching TV and fucking each other so they think of death. I would too. Once, waiting for *Baywatch*, I saw a whole night of some rubbish show called *Sign Field* and I could have killed myself then and there. Four people (not even famous) drinking coffee and talking shit about some soup. The audience was laughing. People told me it was a huge hit but that's why US culture is totally fucked—they've lost touch with basic humour.

We get housewives of a lot of varieties—bored, being cheated on, being cheated on and bored, cheating, usually in the infidelity space. As Brad had predicted (shit, I need to pay him and respond to that Paypal warning), we do get homos sometimes. The main complaint is that US hetero people don't understand them. No issues here. If they pay the per-minute rate, Rashmi is usually deeply understanding of that for three minutes.

When I started this business, I thought we would get a lot of poor people just giving up. Imagine it man. If I was poor and the winter is four months over there, I would see snow and minus eight degrees and no home and think, time to go boss. But interestingly, most of the clients are rich. Rich and betrayed by someone—brother, child, country, hopes. On the 19th, they were betrayed by their portfolio manager.

Here's what the hysteria was like.

7:04 am Eastern Time. Montclair, New Jersey:

'They said my mortgage was fixed.'

Meghan: 'Did you read the fine print sir?'

Gunshot.

9:09 am Eastern Time. New York:

'I don't want the Securities and Exchange Commission to find out about my other trades.'

Greg: 'I won't tell them, sir.'

Jump.

9:11 am Eastern Time. Hyde Park, Chicago: 'Holy fucking shit! NYSE's fallen 200 points in four minutes.'

Greg: 'Sir, put NYSE on the phone. I need to speak directly to the client.'

Car crash.

9:13 am Eastern Time. Greenwich, Connecticut: 'How could I lose five billion dollars in four seconds?'

Meghan: 'That is careless, sir. I've never lost my wallet. Now—'

Stroke.

9:23 am Eastern Time. Park Avenue: 'It's not my fault. I just built the black box. I am a Sri Lankan financial engineer. I am not a criminal.'

Greg: 'Sir, you are not. Instead, let us discuss the spin bowling of Mutthaiah Murlidharan.'

Drowned.

And the day (night) carried on like that. I cannot understand how a civilization—the world's greatest—would give up so easily when the market crashed. These things happen man. So some mortgages were messed around with. So? Harshad Mehta sold stocks he didn't even own and he died of natural causes nursed by a doctor paid for by the government. The same day I had my third tax raid, I discovered that the companies my broker had invested in did not exist. They were all names of his family members.

Luckily, I lost so much money that the IT department ended up giving me money instead of sending me to jail but it was close. And the day it happened, I didn't give up. I didn't say, 'Oh, market has tanked, so where is the gun?' (I know where it was. Antara took it. Why she bought bullets for it, I'll never know, but anyways...) In business, money comes and goes, inflow and outflow, and when it goes—this is a very important lesson—you need a good lawyer. Granted, that would mean even more money will go but eventually, if you find the right white person and match it with the right PowerPoint, it will all come back. Everything is a cycle. And when the cycle is against you, you don't get run over by it. That's the lesson. Under any circumstance, death is pointless. Death doesn't mean Abhudaya Bank forgives your 11 percent EMI. No matter how well you know Regional Cashier, Mr Sunand.

We took 143 hits that day. Non-stop. I don't blame my duo. They are not financial services professionals. After this happened, I did two things. First, I sent Ramesh to get *Buffet on Buffet*—the greatest book ever written on investing in the US markets—just to explain to them what value investing meant. That idiot came back with a book on food. Second, yes, I will admit for the first time here, in print, when they print it on paper, that I got Bhola to delete all the call records of this day. Sorry Sarah. I reported it as Indian Independence Day Holiday but actually, that's August 10 and this was a full working day that

I wasn't proud of. I thought best to show day off than day of 143 dead.

It was really hard, I am sure, for the bereaving families but not as hard as it was on me. It took me months to negotiate with VSNL to prove that we had not made these calls because we could book no profit against it. That night, I watched *CNBC* and read *Wall Street Journal* and cried, knowing there was a market exploding before me and I could do nothing to help them at two rupees a minute international bulk dial rates. As the great movie star Tom Cruise says in the classic *Top Gun*, 'I called, you hung up'. On September 19, 2008, Wall Street called, I hung up.

Performance review

I forgot to tell you about the performance review. I would have done it the day after our chillaxing at Club Poison but I didn't know then how long bail takes. And I didn't know that Antara was in Brazil. Look, the thing is, I didn't know that the gentleman I took the murgh tikka from was the son of the Chief Minister of Maharashtra. He could have said to me, 'Listen man, don't take my murgh. I am the CM's son'. But he didn't. Like a sly fucker, he called the police.

And if Bawa's waiters were more responsive, I would have waited instead of taking it from another table. And the charge that I started throwing chicken at his mother, the CM's wife, is totally untrue. I have never thrown chicken at anyone. Also, it's a twenty-four hour coffee shop, so why wasn't anyone there to take my order?

Three days in prison is not bad. In fact, importance in the business world is directly correlated to days in prison. Price Waterhouse partner during Satyam scam—six months, Reliance Infocomm CEO—four months, me—three days. All it shows is that I have a long way to go in life to be someone important. It will take a lot more hard work. In other countries, going to prison is bad for business. Here, not going is. In other countries, laws are sensible and practical and easy to follow. Here, following the law will get you arrested many more times than breaking it will. Every culture is different. Anyway, I'm not a lawyer though I know it intimately. I often tell my lawyer Suhash, 'You don't know anything', and he laughs and says, 'That might be Gupta. But the way we showed that Swiss transfer would be illegal in any country'. He's a real joker and a good friend. Trouble was, that night he was in jail himself in Pune on some land-for-cow-dung scam.

I had to wait for Antara's return from Brazil to sign thc bail papers. I'm taking a loan to pay her off for the bail... Anyway, like I said, personal life is not important. Performance reviews had to be done back in the office. That was what was important. Not me getting carried away on a Saturday during an offsite.

I take these very seriously. Without performance reviews, there's one major problem that might occur—you might not know how an employee is doing and more importantly, the employee might not know if he/she works there. I saw a Hollywood comedy once called *Office Space*—which I didn't find very funny—where an employee burns down the office because someone takes away his stapler and moves him to the basement. The logic in the story was that he was fired years ago but was still getting his pay cheque. When some consultants (I don't want to say much here about them but my next book is called *Eat, Pray, Fuck Consultants*), fixed the glitch and stopped paying him, he burnt down the whole place. Now I think the main problem here was not the pay cheque. It was performance reviews. If people did yearly performance reviews, we'd know if he worked there or not. There would be no need for arson.

Lazy people do reviews at the end of the year. I do them at the end of every call.

Right after I recovered my car from Powai Lake, I focused on the reviews.

Rashmi was first.

'Can I come in, sir?'

'Wow. Fucking A. Like *Sex in the Citay…Sex in the Call Centrrre…* What happened here?'

'Sir, I went to Millionaire boutique in Juhu. Vasco said in the West, this is business formal.'

'You look…yeah.'

'Sir, you like?'

'Reminds me of Jemma Jemison in *Dirty Office I.* Before she, you know, she takes off… anyway, time out. See that poster? Who the fuck is that?'

'Sir, Barack Obama?'

'No chicklet. Every black man in a poster is not Barack Obama. That's Kobe Bryant. The mofo of basketball. I'm getting into basketball. Knicks, Spurs. A long shot. Watch…'

I had set up a mini basketball court in my room. Obviously.

'Slam dunk!'

'But shouldn't it go in?'

'Whoa. Time out. You know what time out means?'

'Madame Anne said it's saying *give me a break man* but with hands.'

'Not exactly. Here, take this voucher. Go to that Croma store, ask for Goldie and get a Sony Play Station. You and Ramesh should play Play Station basketball at least three hours a day. Next time I see you, I want to dribble you. *And he dribbles past Stockton, the tough guy reserve for San Antinio Spurs...*'

'Sir, you asked to meet me.'

'Yeah, Meghan, I'm promoting you.'

'No, sir!'

'Yes, sir. He says and shoots...'

Thing is, you may ask what does it mean to promote someone in a company of three where one is the boss forever? Nothing. But that's not important. What's important is the feeling.

'Wow. I... thanks. Thanks a lot. Really?'

'You don't know Rajesh, but he's a guy. I was going to promote him in the suicide team because he helped pop star Elton John crawl out of a piano. I don't know how Elton John got into the piano in the first place but you know what I mean. Anyway, time out. Rajesh, he died.'

'What?'

'Yeah he fell into a manhole—floods and all...dead.'

'Oh no. I'm sorry to hear that, sir.'

There was no Rajesh. I made up the story. Always make the employee feel dispensable, especially if they are not. If they think I might bring in someone else, they will believe it and eventually, I won't because there was no one there. I do it to Bhola also. Sometimes I get another person to randomly come in and cook my food and he doesn't know what to do. Insecurity is good. Sadly, you can't do it with your wife. I never tried the insecurity tactic with Antara. Maybe I should have had someone in my bed when she came home from Big Bazaar. Maybe she wouldn't have left me.

'And so now you dress like Hilary Clinton…you can be Hilary Clinton. Ha ha ha…not really. This is your salary increase…tonight, you, Ramesh… *uh-huh, uh-huh, uh-huh, get dirty, get crazy, get some, uh-huh.*'

'Sir, I'm very sorry to say this, sir, but something has got into Ramesh. I don't know if he spoke to you at Club Poison. From two days, he is disturbing me on the phone late at night with crazy talk about breaking my bed. And then today, at Barista, at 8 am, sir, he…I can't talk about this, sir…please tell him to stop.'

'No, you like it? You like it? You're enjoying it?

'A little bit.'

'Yes. Yes. That's it. Nothing wrong with it Napoleanita! It's new India. Sex is healthy. You're in your twenties. Without sex, you'll go mad or catch fire or join politics. When you get in-laws, they might force you to have a child. Wake up, Feminism biatches! If your mother-in-law says get pregnant, you call me. I'll tell her who'll get pregnant. Like see, I told my wife Antara, you can work babymunchkinpuff. You have my permission. Not too much. Maybe interior design. Maybe two hours a day. That keeps her fashionable. If you just eat and sleep, you end up looking like Jaws. I don't want a big shark, I want a wife. So hump a lot tonight, engage in wild things and congratulations. I told you I won't pay you a bonus. I will pay you a bonus per call. Anyone can *earn* a bonus, you have to *deserve* it. You've deserved it. And you've been promoted in your first week. So here it is.'

'I—'

'Yes, yes, you are welcome. But look at your performance. Long shot! You are the best performer in the Suicide Team. One call, one save. That's a 100 percent objective met.'

'Sir, this is four rupees.'

'Yes. Three more than I originally planned. I trebled it, in my mind.'

'Sir, every other call centre is paying a regular salary of Rs 25,000 a month. If I go to Alcoholics or Drug Recovery, it's Rs 30,000. I came to Suicide because I'm into people and helping Americans not die is good no? And I thought on a per call save business I would make at least Rs 50,000 a month.

That's why. But if I get only this much, I can go to TicketMaster Complaints or Marriott Reservation… they will double my…'

'Listen Hilary…'

'I'm the best you have. Who else do you have as good as me? You think Mumbai is short of American BPOs?'

Sometimes an employee will get aggressive but someone like me who's seen the world keeps his cool. There's clearly a disagreement of how much she deserves to get paid. She says fifty thousand. I say four rupees. It is not a tough gap to bridge if you're a pro like me.

'You know what my hero Donald Trump said? He said *Fuckin…A. Fucking…B. Who are you to fuck with me?*'

'I'm leaving, sir.'

'Platinum Dinner for three at TGI Fridays? Deluxe mocktails and free ride on indoor Ferris wheel?'

'No.'

'Pioneer Plasma TV?'

'How many inches?'

'Twenty three.'

'Thanks, no.'

'And video iPod.'

'Um…no. We have.'

'Six months, no-frills, masti magic work out at Gold's Gym?'

'Not interested, sir. I don't have a track suit.'

'Fun Republic Bowling Alley and Prasad's Magic

Palace Video Game Arcade—Family Life membership? And discount coupon for Papa John's Pizza next door? Monthly?'

'Sir, other call centres are giving all this.'

'Kaya Skin Clinic free upper lip hair removal?'

'That I can pay for.'

'Lower lip?'

'No.'

'Chin?'

'Um…no.'

'Family holiday in Bangkok? Free continental breakfast and one complimentary massage? Sightseeing to Golden Buddha not included.'

'Family holiday in New York. Two-star hotel with pool. Shopping voucher and sightseeing to Niagara Falls.'

'Fine.'

'Thank you, sir.'

'Rashmi, are other call centres actually giving better things? You can tell me, I won't take back this offer.'

'No, sir. I just said to bargain.'

'I'm proud of you Clinton. My favourite *chickolate*. See, I grew up in an India with no cell phones. Only Doordarshan. Where power was rationed and water came once a week. I built this to get out of that India. You know what you young people don't realize is that what you take for granted in this country now, is all less than five years old. Your luck will run out.'

'No, sir, don't worry. God bless America.'

I know what you're thinking. Where did she get the balls? But that's new India—so much confidence. Even though they are 12, 16 year olds. No experience. Demanding. From four rupees to an all expense paid holiday to USA. Now I know many negotiations I could have maneuvered, like Formula 1. I could have head-butted her out of 1888 (metaphorically), like a BPO Zidane. But I didn't. Thing is, I need her. I can see her potential, like Gavaskar was picked up by Sir W.G. Grace, like that. In the future, once she comes back from the US, not only will she save thousands of lives, she might even increase the US population. That's my bet. Giving her a trip now is like investing in the BSE at 8000 levels. It will go up.

Then you're probably thinking, what an expense for the business. Total business expense from everything I offered her—zero. These were all things sitting around in my flat. I was trying to get rid of them anyway. Yes, I was going to maybe use some of them, like the Kaya Skin Clinic one, but sometimes business is more important and you have to spend your personal things and bring it into the business. I was reading about Peter North, CEO North Pole Productions, biggest porno video company in the world (Listed NYSE: NPLE). He started with one Sony Handycam, one bed, and his sister-in-law. Today, his market cap is seven billion. So you have to sacrifice something of your own. I was fine with not going on the Ferris wheel or Gold's Gym. Sad, but fine. The Bangkok trip was the one we never took because Antara slapped me and got off the Thai flight leaving me with Fluffer, our Alsatian. When she left me though, she took him too.

The New York trip was that surprise one, which was supposed to be on our anniversary when I came home and found her with…anyway, the point is, sending Rashmi to US didn't cost 1888 anything, even though it may appear I lost the contest.

Granted her bravery left me a little pissed. I encourage my employees to speak their mind and when they do, I realize I shouldn't have let them. Ramesh was next.

Club Poison's events were giving me a throbbing headache. Still—four days later. Some people call it a hangover. I agree with that. It felt like a whole stone was hanging over my face, and it could drop anytime.

'Sir, what do you think, sir?'

He was shouting.

'Why are you shouting you fool?'

'Sir, I am not.'

Probably the hangover.

'Sir…your thoughts?'

'On what?'

'Charagh Din, sir. I went to the showroom and asked for Deboo Comu. I told him CD Rocks, as you said. You also wearing?'

'No way, I've *upgradified*. In life, you got to keep going up, or you'll never be able to look down. This is Reed & Taylor—I've now bonded with the best. Do you know why I called you?'

'Sir, there is a question. Yesterday I got call from this Britney Spears, Los Angeles in bathtub—drowning case—I started laughing. I said why would Britney Spears want to die? She is a dancer. Today, *Bombay Times* headline was "Britney Spears Tries to Commit Suicide". Sir, do you think it's the same person?'

If Ramesh is reading this, I'm sorry I slapped you, grabbed your collar and threw you to the ground. But sometimes performance reviews can be harsh. I've heard that at Goldman Sachs, fifty people have to give their opinion of you.

'Fucker, three days have gone by, and your record is—five calls, two deaths, and three disconnected.'

'Sorry, sir, please don't hit me.'

'It's time for a home run. Where is my baseball bat?'

'Sir, I don't like this baseball game. I like IPL.'

'I'm not playing baseball. I'm going to shove this up your ass.'

'It is not my fault, sometimes I am not understanding them and, sir, most of the customers in USA are mad when they call. They are in some wild crazy mind because normal people will not think of the dying. One said, "I am rubbing a horse" and one more said "I like to sit on a huge inflatable cock" and a third asked if "I like to be having cornflakes with the midgets". I am not following all this, sir. This was not in training. So how I will calm them down?'

'What did I waste dollars to teach you? Are you asking questions like Brad and Anne said?'

'Yes, sir, yes…'

'You are asking, "What are you doing now? What is your favourite thing?" Are you reminding, reassuring?'

'Yes, I ask all that. But I don't know what happens. One person, a black, he had called after he had a bullet in stomach. Now tell me, what I will do there? It's already too late no? I can never win that customer because from the beginning, he is not customer, he is dead. I don't want to die, sir. I have just bought a Nokia N Series.'

'Once upon a time, I used to try to hit on Oshiwara chicks from Hindi serials. I used to eat the midnight buffet at The Marriott. I wore Charagh Din. Then business picked up and I said, time to get higher. Today, the new me, I only hit on chicks from NDTV or Times Now. Yesterday I was invited for an invite only Smirnoff party at Henry Tham's. Are you smelling me? Smell me. What are you smelling?'

'Cologne, sir.'

'Aramis. From Dubai. Musk. When I enter a room, people realize I'm there because they can smell me. In life, you have to keep moving. Nobody will remember you if your smell has faded. Look at you, just a chut in a yellow shirt with no smell of your own. Nobody gives a shit about trying. Anyone can struggle, but can you win? The world remembers only people who claimed their places. They force you to remember them. Everyday, eight million people take trains, no one cares. But some lucky ones get to be in a Merc with a DVD player. Some get an obituary with a colour photo in *Outlook*. Who will you be when you die bastard? Someone in a Charagh Din shirt, cremated by four people or someone who left some smell in the world?'

'Smell, sir. Smell.'

There was nothing more to say. Sometimes if you have a troublesome employee, like that guy at Societe Generale who stole seven billion of their trading money, you can send them to jail. I don't believe in that. I believe in a small thrashing, no salary and a pep talk. Always works. It's what they do in Guantanamo. After that, there is a remarkable improvement in the prisoners. The ones that survive.

Changes in personal life

Among all the things going on, I had forgotten that target I had set for Ramesh against which he was being measured—keeping Rashmi sexually satisfied. Ramesh was to give me regular reports of how it was going.

I told Ramesh to keep notes. The notes are below:

> Sir,
>
> I want to say that I was unsuccessful in the task you assigned to me. But it is not my fault, sir. I was disturbed. You had once said that sometimes in business, you are dependent on suppliers who bring you parts and they fail you. It was something like that.
>
> I went to her flat in Wadala. Pegasus 2C. Her mother had gone to the St Mary's Sports Day even though she had retired as the KG Assistant Principal there in 1999. Apparently, she goes every year. As you would say, sir, the opportunity for my assignment was 'low-hanging fruit'.

We had this 'mood lighting' as you had instructed. She put her two red kaftans on the lamps so it was a proper red light area. Earlier, it was a living room. I don't mean red light area to be funny or clever, sir, so please don't hit me. We put the laptop at a ninety-degree angle and I entered wearing underwear as discussed. I took the dog position. Just like you had drawn it sir. Rashmi was in light purple lingerie courtesy Millionaire boutique. She said something about lace that I did not understand. Maybe it was shoe related but I had taken mine off because they have a Saraswati temple area in the kitchen. Then she brought out the whip. Thank you for giving it to her, sir. We clicked on the folder you said—*Dirty Mistress 3*—and played the mpeg file. The file was corrupted, so we tried another that was called *Beauty on the Beast.* I apologize that we deviated from instructions, sir, but I promise you we did our best to copy. She climbed on top of me and started some light whipping. I must say, sir, that even though it sounds like I'm praising myself, and even though I said 'ow' and 'ah' and 'ogugugugu', I remained in your position. You had said, sir, one the most important business lessons was perseverance. If anything, sir, Rashmi was not whipping properly and I said, referring to activity in the mpeg file, 'Look how she is doing it, do it like her, do it properly no,' and she said 'I am doing it properly but she is on a real horse and that's not a whip. Arun sir will understand.' I was going to respond, sir, but that's when aunty came in.

We jumped behind the—they have a divan, sir, I don't know how to explain in American—sofa. I also had presence of mind, sir. I took the laptop with me. I am not sure what aunty would think of the USB.

'Shit.' I said.

'Fuck. Hide, Ramesh!'

'I thought you said aunty was at her school sports day.'

'Just hide.'

So I hid. It is difficult for me to explain the next set of actions, sir, but what happened was that aunty put on the DVD—*Carmen Electra's Horny Music*—and started dancing. Pole dancing. Aunty was very good. It looked like some other things I had seen on your USB.

Rashmi decided to shut off the CD and talk to aunty.

'Mama, what's happening?'

'Nothing.'

'What are you doing?'

'Sports day gave me a backache so…'

'Were you pole dancing?'

'No! Shut up! What's wrong with you?'

'Why are you on top of the pole then?'

'I was pole climbing. For arthritis, Dr Wagle

advised me to walk uphill. There is no hill in Wadala, so I was going up this pole.'

'You're lying.'

'Yes.'

'There was no sports day was there?'

'No.'

'So where were you?'

'I told Mrs Bodhikar about the pole. She told me pole dancing is getting very popular. Mrs Lobo and Mr Hosham go every Wednesday but they tell their husbands they are playing rummy. The class is in Colaba. Run by a woman called Miss Devine but I think he's really a man called Girish. Today was my first class.'

Then I lost control of the laptop mute button, sir, and it started saying, 'Fuck me like a horse daddy…'

Aunty heard it and said, 'Who is that?'

'No one.' Rashmi tried to brush it off.

'Is that Ramesh?'

I did not know what to do so I emerged from behind the divan. 'Hello aunty.'

'Why aren't you wearing any clothes?'

'I get very nervous in the evenings, aunty.'

'What were you two doing?'

'Nothing, aunty. We were just watching a movie.'

'What movie? Dirty movie?'

'Ha ha, aunty. You're funny.'

Here the laptop went off again, sir. 'Oh yeah, harder, harder…'

'It's on a USB, aunty, I can return it. Our boss recommended watching this to improve efficiency. It's work related. Homework on US culture.'

'Last night there was such a loud noise that Mr Kapoor thought we had bought a dog. Today, the maid found a condom in the microwave and now this. What is going on in this house, Rashmi?'

Sir, aunty's reference to those two incidents were my two previous failed attempts. I brought that Trojan super strength XXL as you said but again, aunty came back from the bazaar so I had to put it in the microwave. The noise was me falling off the bed. I couldn't see her in the dark. Turns out she was not in the room. Wrong jump.

'You're doing item numbers in the living room—that's what's going on in this house, mama.'

Now Rashmi was taking a strong stance. In lingerie.

'You brought this thing into the house, Rashmi.'

'Why do you try things you don't understand? *Carmen Electra's Horny Music* is aerobics exercise. For what you were doing ma, even Celina Jaitley would charge double.'

This was clearly now almost at fight level. Indian actresses were entering the conversation.

'The teacher explained this is like Baba Ramdev's exercise but with a pole. Pole yoga.'

Maybe what aunty was saying was true sir. I have not seen enough Baba Ramdev.

'You don't know anything mama. I'm going to America on holiday.'

'What?'

'Aunty, Statue of Liberty, Disneyland, Hollywood, Levis, White House, GAP, Niagara Falls...'

I explained in case aunty is not familiar with the main attractions of the USA.

'Ramesh, shut up.'

I was almost getting into a mother-daughter fight sir, and I have never done that. My mother died when I was young and I am a boy. So I had no experience in the matter and was learning through the crisis.

'I got a prize from office.'

'You're not going out of this city alone.'

Aunty is definitely a stronger personality than my father sir. For example, her eyes get quite angry. I was scared.

'I've already applied for my visa.'

'Imagine what you'll do in America!'

'Aunty, I'll be in Vashi. Rashmi's going alone.'

'Then imagine what you'll do with foreigners.'

'You will?'

'Have some decency mama, you're an Indian widow.'

'She is a twenty-first century Indian widow.'

I had to clarify here, sir.

'Ramesh, wear some pants.'

'Aunty, you really dance well.'

I expressed how I felt, sir.

'Shut up.'

I will try again, sir. Please have faith.

Okay I almost had it with Ramesh. Anywhere else, like at Yahoo, they would have cut his balls off, but I am not like that. I don't throw people into the mine without food and water and expect them to get me diamonds. I call Ramesh at home late at night. Some people believe that after performance reviews, an employee should be left alone to perform till the next review. I believe he should not. I also believe that life is an ongoing twenty-four by seven performance review. That's what everyone in the business world doesn't understand. I do.

'Charagh Din, I'm watching you.'

'Sir, today I failed to demonstrate your USB to Rashmi but tomorrow is a fresh day no?'

'Fresh night.'

'Yes, night.'

'Tonight.'

'Yes tonight...I meant tonight.'

'You're going to be absent tonight?'

'No no...'

'Because if you are, I'll come to your slum in Vashi and burn it down.'

'Sir, I understand I am on last warning. Please forgive me, I…Hello? Hello?'

I do that sometimes. Become quiet. People think the line is disconnected but I am still there. In my last three businesses, I often did it on conference calls with Sarah and her boss when she asked, 'What is the current status of our investment?' It is a business tactic, very useful during negotiations. See, when the whole Richard Nixon thing happened, I was young but I understood the benefits of wire tapping. This is like that but there is no cost. Nothing to tap into, but the result is the same. Listening to other people secretly. My idea is original. I don't even know why I am writing down this tactic. Maybe Infosys will steal it on their conference calls.

I didn't spy only on Rashmi's house. Favouritism is not my thing. I spied on both houses equally. Daily. In Ramesh's, there were added financial pressures. That's what happens with teenage sisters. Luckily, it didn't start with a pregnancy like I was expecting.

'Anjali found a boy.'

Like I said, 'found a boy' is better than 'having a boy'. See how a change in preposition can change everything? It's the same thing with any business contract. Always read between the lines and above and below the lines also (between the lines is not that important).

'What?' Ramesh gagged with surprise.

'Tell Ramesh the whole thing, papa. I'm in love.'

I know what you're thinking. Even I was shocked that someone would want to marry Ramesh's sister. Where have the standards of marriage fallen? Where does this stop? Next, zoo animals will be on shaadi.com.

'Ramesh, she's claiming everything is set for marriage. December. I checked the date. It's auspicious. Hari Baba says twenty-third is the best. That day Venus is sitting in Saturn's lap, being slowly touched by Neptune. The exact time is 1 am. If that's what she wants.'

'What is going on here, Anjali? You can't decide this stuff without talking to me,' said Ramesh.

'Um, yes I can. And it's not that sudden okay. This morning, I set my Facebook status to "Anjali is looking for husband today" and this one really, really cute guy responded. Finally. And it's his real profile pic. He's been flirting for three hours straight. We both skipped lunch.'

'Who is he, Anjali?'

'Event manager for Harshad's Sexy Events. Works in Pune. Not like your suicide thing. He works during the day—nine to five.'

'No, I mean, what's his name?'

'I forgot. No. Wait. Girish. No. Varun. Varun Govind. But online he calls himself Wild G Thang. I find that hot.'

'So after that you spoke to him? Met him? Have an appointment to meet? What?'

'I wrote on his wall. He's really nice. I said hello, he immediately said hi. I said what brand t-shirt are you wearing? He said Reebok, naturally. So automatically I knew he was cool. Then I threw a virtual sheep at him. He wrote "ouch" on my wall. I said "meow" then "grrr". That's what's been going on all morning. My last message said, "How many children are we having?" He hasn't responded. I think he's religious.'

'Why don't you meet him for a coffee?' said Ramesh.

'I don't want to spoil it. Our love right now is perfect on broadband.'

'Ramesh, as the parent, my view is meeting for coffee will only lead to more trouble. What if she tells this prospective that the teenager who brought out the ad last month in *Mumbai Mirror* offering a nude Internet show to motivate Lok Sabha MPs was her? Not only will we lose this young man, you might get a customer for your suicide hotline. If this marriage does go through, I can pay for…zero. Nothing. The government just put my retirement in a fifty year SBI fixed deposit. We are only on year three. I'm just telling you so you know my position on this matter. I had no idea someone would be willing to marry her this fast. I had no idea *anyone* would be willing to marry her.'

'I am very romantic around 7.30 in the evenings, papa. Just ask people on Orkut. Sharadbradpitt37 is online right now. Ask him.'

'See, Ramesh, I don't even understand what she says.'

'Anjali, as your brother, I think this makes no sense.'

'But, beta, if someone is willing, we shouldn't lose the candidate no? He is Indian, breathing, alive, not in jail. Owns a computer, so clearly he must have electricity. What more can we ask for with Anjali? And if she can't have him, she's threatening to…'

'…auction myself on baazi.com.'

'See? So, Ramesh, you will arrange the money if this goes through, yes?'

'And I want a Ritu Kumar dress.'

'Huh?'

'You said you'll pay for the Malad flat and the new Hyundai. Just change that to a big wedding at Orchid,' said Old.

'What?'

'No, Ramada bhaiya!' squealed Anjali.

'Ramada?'

'Plus add plane tickets for all relatives from Bhopal. They will have to come no.'

'How much will Shekhar Suman charge for an appearance, papa?'

'Not much. Maybe three…'

'…thousand?' Ramesh now began to perspire profusely.

'Lakhs! Let me get in touch with the boy's family immediately,' said Old.

'Please say yes bhaiya...please say yes...please... please...'

'YES!' said Ramesh, who had clearly given up on hope by now.

In my thirty years as a business leader and India Inc. ambassador, I have never seen such a tense fundraising effort. Except once, while watching the great guru Arindam Chaudhary asking people in Indore to fund a business school he wants to start exclusively for Indians in Las Vegas. This was like that.

Notes from battle. Part deux (That's Roman).

All wars have stories. That's why the term 'war stories'. You can tell that I've avoided the obvious cliché and called it Notes From Battle. And because it's the second one, I didn't say Part II (obvious) but Deux, which means 'two' in Roman.

See, there's an important lesson here. Sometimes in business, you will make a product just like someone else's product or you'll do something that has an established name and is done by everyone, like 'manufacturing', 'urinating', 'having a coffee break', 'stealing source code'. But to differentiate, to make your thing or you look different and better than the mundane thing that everyone's doing, call it something else. For example, instead of manufacturing, say 'assembling' (doesn't matter if assembling means something else), for 'urinating' say 'letting it flow', and for stealing say 'working late'. At worst, it will confuse people, or they will correct you and say, 'This doesn't mean that, you fool'. At best, they will think you are an innovator.

Bill Gates often talks about innovation being the creation of something new. I disagree. That's why he is where he is, in some slum outside Bangalore peddling AIDS vaccines and I am where I am. Here. In battle. So who would know more, a soldier in the trenches of modern business or some NGO guy trying to save HIV-infected African children? Don't answer that. My message to Bill is simple. I show up on Z Business during working hours while he shows up on BBC at night asking for donations. Let the public decide what that means for business credibility.

Ergo (innovated word for 'therefore'), innovation doesn't have to just be limited to new things. Just a new word is enough. If you had the Coca Cola formula and made your own soft drink called Aloc Acoc, that's fine, that's innovation, that's Coca Cola spelt backwards. As long as you can manage their lawyers, you can have a thriving business.

That's why I innovated a better title than 'war stories'. And if you can, go into another language, like I went into Roman for a replacement of 'Part two'. No one speaks Roman anymore but *deux* sounds old and when you think of the word, you picture a Roman soldier in a helmet and a sword. So you think this person must either be really old (no) or really knowledgeable about history (which I am). See what I am doing with innovation here? Planting new thoughts. These are the seeds to ideas that could one day become Monsanto, the world's largest seed company. And that's just with one chapter title.

The second part of a battle is always harder because you have finished half the battle and are tired (fear of returning to mother tongue accent) but our second part was not just harder, it changed everything.

Just like discovering, after fifty years of smooth Coca Cola production in an assembly line, there's one bottle of Pepsi, or finding a small human thumb in a frozen tray of Sainsbury's chicken makhni, these calls changed the course of our business forever. And my life.

Call Log

Time: 4 am
Date: December 4, 2008
Duration: 4 minutes.

'Hello.'

'Listen Hilary, Arun here, I'm sorry to disturb your vacation but I'm not really sorry. It's a special case, everyone feels only you can handle it—can I connect you?'

'Sir, I just got to the hotel. Two days late. The Air India flight had to reroute because of some non-payment thing so we had to fly to Cairo. All we had to eat was this thing called cream cheese bagel, sir.'

'Chicmagnet, when Alexander was told to fight a war, did he say he was eating a cream cheese bagel? And bagel is pronounced Beaujolais.'

'Sir, they are saying Manhattan is very far from this hotel. And you said hotel but this is a Super 8 Motel. They are saying this is New Jersey. Two hours away.'

'They don't know anything. And in the US, a Super 8 Motel is better than a hotel. That's why the "super" in the name. If you live there, you would know. I have given you a room in the best place. You are at the city centre. Times Square is two minutes if you change a few buses. If you look from the top floor, you can see the Empire State Building.'

'Sir, there is a highway that I can see from my room, 330. It says Pennsylvania 20 miles. And I can see room 331.'

'Maybe your room is facing the wrong way. Anyway, this is a Code Special Alert Case. I was about to trace the location and call the police because I am a genius but then my brain is smarter than me. It said to me, this is the chance for Rashmi to wear my Reid & Taylor suit. So this is your chance. If you can't, no one can.'

'Fine. What's the case?'

'He is a fucked-up deude who is locked up in a hotel room saying stupid things like "I am a fucked-up deude". Mad guy.'

'Okay, sir. Let me speak to him. Transferring... Thank you for holding, sir. Mr Bin Laden, you are now talking to Meghan. She is our expert. She can help you.'

'Hello? Suicide Watch, this is Meghan.'

'My name is Osama Bin Laden. I was born in Yemen. I founded a company called Microsoft. Later,

I became the first African American President of the United States. I also freed Palestine and discovered the Internet. I have the formula for Coca Cola. On Sundays, I fart and oil comes out—800 million barrels that will fuel all the world's cars.'

'The world thanks you for doing this. Where are you now, Mr Laden?'

'In a motel. I hate motels.'

'Ha ha ha. Me too.'

'You find that funny? You know what else is funny? Asians. They're so rich now, the Chinese—Ali Baba.com—do you know it? It is like China's Google. And the Indians. Who the hell thought huh? Red curry to customer service? Do you know all calls for anything now go to India? How crazy is that? Like how to operate your cable or microwave or finding a funeral home? Bombay Fucking Palace, that's what the place was called. In Albany. Little asshole there with a moustache. Smelt like shit. Gaurav. He rules the world now. Doesn't need to do namaste to me. Doesn't need to feed me naan fucking bread. Fuck the Japanese though, they're messed up. Do you know, in Tokyo, they have vending machines for used school girl panties?'

'I didn't know that, sir. Sir, is your hand near your penis? Sometimes, people who are distressed are not that distressed. What you are feeling is perhaps not a life-and-death situation, maybe it is a sexual requirement that you have. I recommend a USB in which you can keep some special films.'

'Do you watch *Seinfeld*? What did you say your name was?'

'Um, Meghan.'

'Meghan, I'm going to ask you three questions about Jerry Seinfeld. If you don't answer them, I will blow myself up like Abu Musab Al Zarqawi. Do you know who that is? You should. He was only 24 years old when he became Al Qaeda's commander in Iraq. They say he was the youngest but the explosives expert they caught in Tunis, Ab Hafs, was 19. He doesn't get much press, Abu Hafs. Even less now that he's dead. But then so is Al Zarqawi and everyone features him. *New York Times.* Like some fucking Hollywood star. The Americans tried to burn him but he burnt himself. Much cooler. Do you ever wonder why Qaeda in Al Qaeda is not spelt with a "u" as all things with Q are, as in the Pakistani city Quetta—qu, or Qualification—qu? But not these guys. They don't say Quaeda (pronounced *kwayda*) but Qaeda (*kaeeda*). It's like they were blowing up the English language too. You know?'

'Sir, you have probably become temporarily mad. I can get help—if you could just—'

'*Second Life*, now that's a super dumb fucking idea. Do you know it? It's like this world on the Internet where you can just fucking live. Like pay rent and stuff and have virtual frappuccinos. You know the accounting firm Accenture? They have a fucking office on *Second Life.* Who is going to get their online life audited? People don't do that in real life. Someone said, "Oh, it's a great way to meet people. Go to a virtual nightclub, grab a beer, say what's up". What? I can barely sit through a polite meal with my family in my first life, why would I want to wait in a long line outside a nightclub that isn't even there? And what if they don't let me in? Look, it is still the same shit world with the same people. I mean will stuff change there? Will I be on *Seinfeld*? You know then I think—I think we will run out of oil and food and water and everything will be destroyed by floods and earthquakes and maybe all we'll have then is broadband and *Second Life*. You ever think of that?'

'No, sir, not very often. In fact, not at all.'

'You know what else? You know you can't just have sex with someone on *Second Life*. They can arrest you if she isn't willing. I mean what the hell is that? Who makes these rules? How do you even know a virtual person is a person? Sending me to fucking *Second Life* prison—the nerve!'

'Sir, is there anyone we can speak to to get you out of prison?'

'Forget that. Here's my first question—what's the name of the film where Jerry Seinfeld played a bumblebee? It's a cartoon. Hello? Are you still there?'

'Rashmi, Arun here, I have put a hold on the line. Clintonista, we've traced call to New Jersey. Should I inform the police or bomb squad?'

'No, sir, no need, he's bluffing, I'm sure.'

'You're sure?'

'Yes sir. He doesn't have a bomb or anything. He isn't in any hotel either. He's in his house wasting time, sir. Lonely person. Trust me, I can tell. I have had many callers like this. In other call centres. One used to call me everyday, naked.'

'Good. I like him. Maybe it's the same guy. Get back on the call.'

'Hello? Nobody keeps Osama holding. Hello?'

'Sorry, sir, the line's unclear, you were saying—'

'Too late. Second question. Jerry Seinfeld ran away with someone's fiancée. What's her name?'

'Sir, is it difficult to be retired and stare at depression tablets? Have you committed a heinous crime on a dog or cat? Have you thought of a bubble bath? Have money market funds destroyed your savings in the recession? How about a holiday for one to New York? I find it very good.'

'Ha! Last question—Jerry Seinfeld wrote the show *Seinfeld* with another comedian who has become really famous with his own show on HBO. What's the comedian name and what's the show called?'

'Sir, maybe if you went down to your local bar and got drunk, you would realize that only *some* people think you're a psycho.'

'You know, Meghan, when all this is over, everyone will thank Osama Bin Laden. No one will call him a psycho. They'll say he started it. And he ended it. I'm going to kill myself now. Goodbye.'

'Sir, don't go, please don't go. Just tell me where you are.'

'It's a cool autumn evening. There's a New Jersey highway under me. Route 12, I think. The road looks so nice and calm and tiny from here. I'm like a God. Above concrete. You know why I don't like hotels? I don't like long corridors with Mark Rothko prints. I don't like Kenny G tunes in elevators. Why would you play that to guests who are spending money on you? Hotels are dead. Hotels are hollow yellow holes for salesmen, fornicators, travelling professionals. Yet, the *New York Times* will report I chose to jump off one.'

'Okay, sir, which hotel are you staying at?'

'It's a Motel 6. Room 331. Owned by some Indians. They own everything in New Jersey. And wear superstitious rings. That's another problem. Wait, I'm climbing out of my window.'

'That's not possible, sir, because I'm in Motel 6 on the third floor—'

For a minute, I heard nothing.

'What happened, Rashmi kebab?'

'I'm watching a man, sir. He is naked and is climbing out of his window. Should I open my window? Sir, could it be—'

'Describe the landscape, Roshomon.'

Without the landscape, no battle can be won. Ask any American. If Tora Bora was not a mountain region in northern Afghanistan and was a palm tree-lined Caribbean island, Americans would have a very different plan.

'Sir, New Jersey is a pretty flat land area, many lakes—'

‘No you fool, the landscape of the hotel. And don’t keep saying motel.’

‘Sir, it *is* a motel. And this man has climbed out of his window. If I climb out of my window, he can see me. We share a long, narrow verandah type thing sir but it is not like a Colaba verandah. It is narrow. Shall I open my window and climb—what should I do?’

‘Oh shit! Yes! Open. Open!’

‘Okay, sir, opening, climbing out. Now—?’

‘Talk to him, chicken nugget. Talk to him. That’s what got you to the US in the first place. Talking to Americans. Now tell Osama to hold and see what is going on here.’

‘Hello. I’m Osama Bin Laden. I am about to kill myself. Who are you?’

Rarely am I speechless. I was then.

‘Sir, he is also saying he is Osama Bin Laden. What is going on in the USA today, sir?’

I was still speechless. But by now, I knew what had happened. Some people are quick at instinct. I am quicker.

Now in life, coincidences will occur. I once saw this movie *Usual Suspects* starring this actor Kevin Spacey. Now the whole movie was the search for a criminal mastermind called Kaiser Soze. Turns out at the end of the movie, Kevin Spacey was Kaiser Soze. Coincidence. No one could have put this one and that one together. That’s the heart of coincidence.

Business example. Genius hedge fund titan Raj Rajaratnam running a seven-billion dollar hedge fund whose essential purpose is talking on phones to get insider information gets indicted for insider trading and the damning evidence is the tapped phone conversations. Coincidence. If you know anything about ISC mathematics, you will know 'probability'. It studies the probability of something happening. And you have to run regressions to determine the probability of something. For example, when my earlier tax issue was going on, I paid an IIT graduate two packets of mutton biryani to run a probability on an IT raid. He said 1 in 132, which was not very high. They are not always accurate. I was raided while he was explaining this to me. Explaining to the IT people why I was running this probability was another adventure.

After this incident, I made Ramesh run three parallel regressions. We are a suicide outsourcing hotline. Chances of meeting people committing suicide were 1 in 1,000. Probability of meeting people committing suicide while on weeklong holiday in the country of the customer? 1 in 100,000. Probability of meeting people committing suicide while on a weeklong holiday in the country of the customer and being on a call with that customer? 1 in a million. Ergo, never.

That's why I hate mathematics. Never works. I go with guts. Except, RBI doesn't print money with gut instinct, and banks don't accept gut instinct as deposits—they do it with currency and mathematics. That's the thing fucking the world and that's what needs to change.

'Jesus, you're facing the client? Same hotel, same floor, he wasn't lying? I had told you, Chicamama, don't go to the US. Fuck. Say something to him. You're my best biatch! DO SOMETHING! Can you distract him? Take off your clothes so he doesn't feel out of place. What are you wearing? Can you hit him? Is there a TV or a phone near you? Throw it.'

There was silence on the other end, and then she said, 'Sir, I don't know what to say.'

'Clintonamera? Hilary Duff? Hello? Tell me something, Chicmango. Anything.'

'He jumped, sir.'

And that's how it happened. That's why I wanted to write down the details. So you could see the thing. So you can see I was innocent. I told you I warned her. I told her don't go. I don't know who else to say this to. Maybe Facebook.

You may say, but Arun, you see everything, how did you not see this? To be honest, I did. Only thing I always worry about is proximity. Sometimes, if you're in sales, it's not a good idea to come in close contact with customers. Face-to-face may cause problems. Anyway, there are 270 million Americans. And Rashmi is one. The chances of coming face-to-face are not high. That's what I thought. Then again, I don't play poker. I have started now.

To say I was surprised would be right. I was surprised. Not that Rashmi would fail me. But that she would fail me in a face-to-face. On the phone, sitting here, I could have tolerated it. Over there, my ticket, my hotel room, easy chance to catch, she drops it. That too after all the training. There were two moments in my life when the world disappointed me and I had too much faith in someone. The first was when all-rounder Imran Khan joined politics. And the second was this.

If you want my reaction to this event, I would say something had to be done. She would come back seeing what dying was and her performance would suffer. My gut was telling me that. I should have shown them dead bodies or something as part of their orientation to what 'failed customer' meant. Just to set expectations. When people get a pay cut, others tell them months in advance to plan. Just one visit to a graveyard would have been enough. In business you have to admit when you are underprepared. If Union Carbide had admitted that they were unprepared then maybe some people in Bhopal would have said 'fine'. I am magnanimous to admit that not showing them the end result would result in this kind of end.

And on top of that, with that fucking fool Ramesh not being able to have basic conversations, we were heading for a crisis worse than when BP's Deepwater Horizon burst.

Call Log

Time: 5.45 am
Date: December 11, 2008
Duration: 4 minutes.

'Madam, my name is Gregory and I want to enquire why you want to put your head into oven?'

'Well, cause I…'

'Can you please tell me about the oven?'

'Like, no. I mean wtf? I'm 13 years old and I realize that I'll never be as hot as Scarlett Johansson. Never. I want to die.'

'Arun sir, Scarlett Johansson is a Hollywood actress no? Which one is she?'

'Blonde.'

That's why my people rely on me. To come in with vital information that will make all the difference. Leading from the back.

'Why do I always get entertainment cases, sir? I don't even like movies.'

'She did one movie…that *Lost*…'

'Sir, lost what?'

'Just say "lost", idiot.'

It's important in any business to be brief and not specific. Too many details spoil the customer.

'Sir, I have told you that we need US entertainment expert.'

Ramesh knows nothing of expense control. There's already one US expert here—me. Why should we pay another person for what I know? That's like having two fans and an AC in your bedroom switched on all the time, when you may be travelling.

'Oh, Ramesh, she was in *Spiderman* also.'

'Sure, sir?'

'No.'

'Madam, Gregory here. Thank you for your patience. Let us, together, try to solve the problem Miss… Miss?'

'Cheetah. Call me Cheetah. I'm Amy, but like the tropical mammal, agile—never intimidated. That's what my friends call me.'

'Remember what Scarlett said in the movie *Lost*?'

'Um…yeah, like every friggin' line. "Evelyn Waugh was a man. Are you in Tokyo alone?" What's your point?'

'You arc gctting an education?'

'I'm in seventh grade. Look, can I just tell you I've done everything for Scarlett. I've got like six Facebook fan sites and MySpace I don't even want to get into and like the postings on Twitter and Bebo. And can I just tell you, her publicist, stylist, manager whatever, I've saved emails from all of them. Like, there are two fan sites for her and like four unofficial and I'm like registered and like a moderator on three of the Yahoo groups. But like what no one knows is that you get her best gossip on the Scarlett Go Die sites. Like there's one that…urghh!!!! I so hate her. You know?'

'Don't cry, dear. I can totally understand your emotion.'

'Dear' was a nice touch. Close to US feelings. I made them watch this American film *Gone with the Wind*, and although I couldn't understand anything they were saying, this one big black person said 'dear'. I think Ramesh picked it up from that movie. They had a Scarlett there also. Ugly. Red hair. Not my scene.

'Scarlettt!!!!!!!! Leave me alone!!!!!!!!! Why are you doing this to me??????? You fucking bitch!!!!!!! Will you love me when I leave a suicide note blaming you? Will you like that, you slut?'

'Madam, Cheetah, do your parents know what you're going to do with the oven?'

'Like, no, I'm not like insane to tell them. They're at a Coldplay concert and they left me with this walnut squash celery thing. Which is another thing I'm mad about. But when I'm dead, they can see how fucked up they were to leave me with this shitty salad. We don't even get the premium channels on cable and no TIVO. What the fuck? I hope they're arrested. I think in London they arrest parents for negligence or whatever.'

'But, madam, you are beautiful in a different way no?'

Nice touch. Massage ego. Nice.

'Like no, have you seen me? I'm not beautiful at all. And I have a shit personality. That's what my friends say. And I don't really care about anything, like student government or model UN or the environment. I don't even want to kill everyone in school. I just want Scarlett to know, do you understand me?'

'Do you want to talk to Miss Scarlett?'

'What? You guys can do that?'

'Yes.'

'Here? Now? Are you kidding me?'

'We have her number. If we tell her what you're about to do, maybe she'll listen.'

'Greg, are you shitting me?'

Ramesh turned to me with a tinge of desperation in his voice. 'Sir, can you do hot blonde voice? Please.'

'No.' To be honest, I tried once at 1-888-Blow-Job but it didn't go too well. The customer said, 'Arun?' It's a long story. And I have a bigger theory about this. When someone has already fallen off a roof and is heading to the street a hundred floors below, it is time to let go. Ramesh was at that time.

'Greg?'

'I am trying Ms Johansson's cell phone right now... please hold.'

'Oh my GOD! Aahhhhhhhhhhhhhh!!!!!!'

'Madam, please control yourself.' He then said to me. 'Where can I listen to Scarlett Johansson, sir? I need to hear her.'

'YouTube?'

'I can't wait for it to download, sir. This Internet speed is...Gmail took three hours to load yesterday, sir. We are still on dial up modem.'

I knew all this. But broadband can't just be bought. It has to be earned. Anyone in any job always complains about Internet speed. But as a manager you have to ask, what have they done to deserve faster Internet? That was my logic. Save lives, increase KBPS. But I didn't give too much away at this point to an employee. A boss must hide while being seen.

'Ramesh, just do an American girl voice. You remember the training, don't you?'

'Greg, you're actually like fucking doing something to get her? She's in Italy shooting for Lars Von Trier.'

'Yes, yes, we have just located her outside Italy… Rome. We are arranging urgently. Please hold. Please switch off the oven.'

'Holy fucking shit.'

'Have you moved away from oven?'

'Yeah, yeah.'

'Ms Cheetah, you will now be connected to Ms Scarlett Johansson. She is busy, you only have two minutes to talk to her. Ms Amy Cheetah, are you there?'

'Yes.'

'Here you go…connecting…Ms Johansson, you're speaking with Ms Amy. Thank you for taking time off shooting for this emergency.'

'Amy?'

I almost said whoa. But that would not have been a good idea given I was not on mute and I listen in on every call. Yes, personal also, especially personal.

As I explained to you before, personal is equal to professional. Anyway, back to the suspense.

This was like watching a movie. My favourite. *Top Gun*. But only sound. Total silence. Like the last scene when you think Cruise is dead.

I have to say though that Ramesh did a good imitation of a girl's voice. Hot teen. That's where my 'whoa' came from. For those who don't get it, 'whoa' means surprise. Seriously though, if your eyes were closed, you could get carried away with the girl Ramesh. If I had this in 1888-Blow Job, I wouldn't have gone bankrupt. In business, this is known as post mortem.

'Yes.'

'Amy, listen to me. This is Scarlett. You have to listen to me, okay? Killing yourself is not going to get you any closer to me, yes? If you want to be my friend, I need you alive. I need you to support my movies and my music and magazines okay? I need you, right now, to STOP anything that will destroy your home, property or yourself. I'm in Rome but I'm going to come to Williamstown and meet you as soon as I'm back okay?'

'I love you. You have no idea how much.'

'I love you too. I have to go now okay? You promise to NOT do anything bad to yourself tonight. You could, instead, watch one of my movies till your folks get home?'

'I promise, Scarlett.'

'Good. I'll send you an autographed DVD of *Lost* okay?'

'Okay, Scarlett. Thank you, Scarlett.'

'I am glad to hear that. I am going now. You'll absolutely promise to behave?'

'I swear. Never again.'

'Okay, bye. Shall I tell 911 to call on you and check?'

'No, I'm going to go to Anne's house and we'll watch *Girl with a Pearl Earring*. You do Renaissance so well!'

'Thank you.'

Sometimes people become greater than what they are. If I was Einstein, I would put it like this—the sum of their parts can't hold the whole of them back. That's really all there is to say on this. And maybe a couple of things more. Think of Churchill when England was losing World War II. He cut down on red meat. Henry Ford invented the assembly line at a time when people liked factories to be in complete chaos. Think of Frank Quattrone, the Credit Suisse investment banker who was going to be put in jail for doing bogus Internet IPOs, and under all that media glare, he refused to shave his big moustache. People can rise to an occasion, like Ramesh rose now. Don't worry, I am not a cheap person. I will not use this opportunity to correlate it to some erection joke. Although I have humour, this is a business memoir. Its purpose is bigger. Like a business Bible. And the Bible doesn't have cheap punch lines.

So I will use this forum to do what all bosses do. Recognize performance. Everything, the voice, Williamstown, *Girl with a Pearl Earring*—he made all that up on the spot. Spectacular. Like the way Imran Khan marries white women. One thing we should all realize in business is that we could not be the pillars of industry were there no building above us to hold up. We would not be leaders were it not for people to lead. Today, or that night, I was proud to lead Ramesh into Scarlett Johansson.

Tenzig Chooha

There is a man I know. Actually, there are many men I know in many important spots—Cabinet, IMF, British Parliament, UN, Tihar jail. But this deude is more important. His main name is Girish Mhatre and he lives in Bhandup but he also goes by the alias Anthony Karnik from Cochin, Yusuf Mohali from Mohali and Ms Devine from Colaba. No, it's not just for crime—he needs it for his different businesses.

Yes, many businessmen are known by the power of their 'Rol-A-Dex' cards as they say in New York (I call it Crap-A-Dex). Business cards that are revolving and show power. It says, 'Look, this card is of someone important, this is another card, someone more important' and so on. It's like a card game but with no climbing stakes, therefore no thrill. This only works if the cards get more and more powerful till you get to God. But that's not likely. Most of the time you can't even get an assistant—you call them and their numbers have changed because they were having an affair or lost their phone in a ditch or were fired. Important contact, bye bye. My Rol-A-Dex is inside my brain area. Sarah VC's private number.

Bhola's panchayat leader's number. Antara's massage guy Thor Ganguly's number. I could go on.

Why? And this is what white people in suits often forget—that the most important people in the world don't have business cards. Does Barack Obama have a business card? Or Aamir Khan for that matter? Thing is, some people don't need to show their power on small white rectangular paper (no matter how hard they try to make it from material that does not tear).

Girish Mhatre was a Maharashtra MLA for Vashi. He needed that name because it is hard to win an election under any other name. Especially for the Shiv Sena. But Mhatre, like me, is a thinker, a doer. He is, in a word, a renaissance man. It's a word I like to use—it means all-rounder. That doesn't mean Ian Botham (cricketer, lover of West Indian chicks) or Kapil Dev (cricketer, Gillette ambassador) were renaissance men. They were just all-rounders. Mhatre was a renaissance man because he also ran a passport operation in Cochin under the name Anthony Karnik. By operation I mean he gave people passports. Now, some people may say it is the job of the External Affairs Ministry to give passports but I tell those people, have you ever stood in line for a legal passport? Have you ever tried filling out one of those forms? I know two people who got heart attacks trying to fill them out and these are government people who created those forms. What kind of a form has a Roman XXVVII subsection in a country where most people can't read Roman? I can because I'm into history. My friend found a business opportunity where people wanted to go to Dubai and had to wait four months to get a passport, so he bypassed the government and made his own. In China, if The Bank of China doesn't like the day's weather, they send a plane to change the clouds so why can't Mhatre become Anthony to make Indian passports in a basement in Cochin? (His wife Joanna helps with the forgery).

Business should be simple. Ed Gillespie who invented the vending machine used to say that all businesses should be like vending machines. Press a button, get a product. Yes, some things may be too large to fit into a vending machine, like an apartment, or a car or a horse but that's because of our engineering limitations of not being able to build a large enough vending machine. The point is simplicity. Business equals cash equals things equals simplicity. Like my business model. Life equals cash. Death equals bankruptcy. In Mhatre equals Karnik's case, cash equals passport. Government passport equals heart attack.

My work with Mhatre, however, was neither with Mhatre nor Karnik. It was with Ms Devine, a Christian lady from South Goa. In this case, Mhatre changed his name and his sex. Some businesses you can do as a man, some as a woman. Ms Devine bought smuggled goods from customs officers and sold them to other smugglers. Commission-based business. He already had two police records as Girish Mhatre and Anthony Karnik, so he thought it best to diversify into this third business as a woman. That's an important business lesson—don't let your sex get in the way of your business idea. Women say that when it comes to rising to the level of CEO of a company, they face a glass ceiling. I look at this as a similar scenario but with a critical difference. For reference, see Coke and Pepsi. I call this a genital ceiling. The core difference, if you take everything else away (maybe this was said by management guru Peter Drucker), between men and women in the workplace, is genitals. Have and Have not. Having and not having should have nothing to do with business. That's my feminist view. If you are into bras or pink scooters or designer stores or hand bags, why do you have to be a woman to start those businesses? Does boob lead to double-digit scooter growth? Why can only men run trucking companies or coal mines? What I say is lose the testicles (or get them) and raise the stock price, that's what investors care about. Lots of chicks like me for this. In fact Kanika slept with me because…I won't get into that here. I will say, she took my advice and is now very senior at HDFC.

Also, what I like about Girish is that Ms Devine's business is an independent vertical. It doesn't compete with passports or elections and nor does he, woman, compete with he, man. That's another good point—if you have many business verticals, you don't have to do all of them as a man. I hope Bajaj and Godrej read this.

Ms Devine was my supplier of phone equipment, computer equipment, original Taiwan products, and she made some profits by smuggling in Q1 that she invested in another very good business idea—a gym. Infinity Gyms Pvt Ltd to be precise, and that turned black money into white. If Ms Devine was a financial advisor in the 1980s, so many Indian businesses would be physically in shape and have money laundered properly without going to Switzerland. The gym mainly focused on pole dancing lessons with lots of South Mumbai housewives as members. It's a great target market—rich women with husbands in export businesses, all with club memberships, at least four of them with HSBC credit cards. Physically obese, body spread out wide, and ignored by the husband who is sleeping with London escorts, they want to regain some dignity by dancing around a pole. Yes, I did take a few lessons but I was too advanced for beginners and then got into advanced. I talked to Ms Devine about teaching also but she said, not now.

There was the pole you know about, the one that Ms Devine gave me for my office. They were presents because she/he did not have skills to get them cleared through customs and I did. First shipment that came in, customs thought they were Stinger missiles. This is the trouble with our customs people—not enough erotic experience. The poles come from Almaty, by the way, in Khazakistan—which has the world's largest number of strippers—so it's authentic and tested. I danced sometimes to think. I read that Cornelius Vanderbilt used to go for long walks to think. I pole danced. Then I gave it to Rashmi. In old British kingdoms, when you handed down your crown or gave someone a large piece of land or some slaves, it was called bequeathing. I bequeathed my pole to the next generation. Every business needs a succession plan. Otherwise, it would be like the Ambanis. In ten years, Rashmi, Ramesh, and I will be pulling at the pole. I wanted to avoid that.

So I was really surprised when I saw two things. First, an old lady with Rashmi's pole in Ms Devine's class doing some really shameful things, and my old school friend, Tenzig Chooha.

I hadn't seen Tenzig in thirty-five years. We were best friends at… (I'm not going to reveal my school. I didn't even tell the CBI. There are reasons). He often asked if I was embarrassed to visit him in his house when we played Lego as children. I wasn't. 'You're shivering,' his mother used to say. I wasn't. Look, it's not like I hadn't gone into duplex flats facing the Arabian Sea before. It may have been the tallest building in Mumbai in 1975 but today, it will fit comfortably inside the DB Realty Orchid Tower, where I plan to book a flat as soon as the promoters are out of jail. Thing is, the four thousand square feet of marble with antique furniture and the Italian crystal chandelier may have been cool in old India but today, even Bhola can buy it (soon). It was just the height that made me shiver. Penthouse. As a child, I was worried we were too close to planes. We were. We still are. I don't know why the BMC doesn't do something about that building—Shalimar

Manzil—it's now some heritage site. I asked someone a few years ago what Tenzig's family building is worth and he said priceless. Everyone knows what that means. Zero. If you can't put a price on something, it's not worth having it because you can't have it. That's what I say.

Thing is, Tenzig and I were very close as long as you didn't believe those rumours about me stealing his Lego castle. And I could never understand why my mother kept asking if he was ashamed to come to our house. We lived lavishly in a one-bedroom in Dongri... The point is, whatever Tenzig is today, in new India, I'm much better off. He didn't have a cook/personal secretary and two employees back then. I do now. That's what matters—not where you started, but where you ended. I saw a film called *Benjamin Button*. Shit. It's about Brad Pitt (who is no Tom Cruise), who ends up with nothing. In a nappy. What's the point of that? That's achievements going backward. The world doesn't want to see Bill Gates going back to school to learn how to type on a PC. The world wants to see Bill Gates become Bill Gates. Business is always fast forward. So is life.

Like I said, I did not shiver from jealousy about where he lived and how many toys he had. He had a lot. And anything you might hear about the principal suspending me on grounds of being a kleptomaniac because I stole his Toblerone and London tiffin box is definitely not true. We had many Arun Guptas and it's a common confusion, as I've explained before. In fact, the police often come and question me about some Arun Gupta smuggling things…anyway.

Some people ask, Arun, how did you manage to go to such an elite school when you were living in that room? One word—connections. Another word—government. Together, government connections. If this were a mathematics equation, I would say government plus connections plus dad a civil servant in the State Education Board minus principal bribe multiplied by principal family threat times two (Rev Suarez had two kids) equals convent school equals India. Every country has an equation. This is ours. It's not a fair equation but mathematics is not fair. Not moral. That's why mathematics drives business and that's why, even though I hate it when compared to gut instinct and even though I hate probability, I like it. As the great philosopher whose name I'm forgetting said, 'It is what it is'.

There is a great legend about Tenzig Chooha. His father, Maximus Chooha, was a renowned gambler and suspected father of many South Mumbai children. On Tenzing's 16th birthday, he informed Tenzig that he had made a slight mistake. He had taken all his savings that were supposed to be Tenzig's inheritance, including Shalimar Manzil and bet it on the 1.30 pm Derby race where the stud Evening in Paris was a 31:2 favourite. The horse apparently ran in the opposite direction, later to be found mad, under the influence of mysterious narcotics causing media speculation about a plot by business rival and carpet magnate Huffington Saldanah.

To summarize, Maximus was bankrupt and Tenzig would have to support the family with a trainee job at Bata posted at the showroom opposite their house on Colaba Causeway. We were ten days away from our ISC finals and Tenzig, at midnight, ran away from home never to be seen or heard of again. In anger, Maximus left the family (Tenzig had a sister and I think, a mother) and started another one, also in Colaba not far away, breaking all ties from his existing one. By the way, I didn't take the ISC exam either—that involves other reasons, something to do with a fire as I hinted at before—but let's get back to Tenzig.

This is the first time I'm seeing him since then.

'Arun Gupta, been a long time since they sent you to jail for taking my—'

'Tenzig, you look the same!'

'So if it wasn't you, did the school ever find out who burnt down the assembly hall?'

I had to change the topic. I looked at the old lady and said, 'That's my pole.'

'My daughter gave it to me.'

'Is your daughter Rashmi?'

'You must be Dr Arun Gupta. Hello sir. My daughter loves you as her boss, sir.'

Yes, I was nominated for an honorary doctorate by Lovely Professional University, Bhopal, but they meant Arun Gupta, Head of Mckinsey India. But how did she know I was doctor?

'You save so many lives. Thank you, doctor.'

'You are welcome.'

Ah. So this was Relentless Aunty. She seemed much kinder in person than the mad shouting "no" lady.

'Your husband knows you dance here?'

'My husband passed away. Rashmi told you?'

'Maybe.' (Never give out information unless receiving equal amounts. Most people think business is give and take. My philosophy is take and take like investment banks.)

'You know, doctor, I may not be as great as you, doing what you are doing, but I used to be a school principal. I've retired now.'

Why thc fuck was she telling me all this, I wondered. It didn't matter. Tenzig was listening and that's what mattered.

'I don't understand my child nowadays. All this cell phone texting, computers. Out all night. I can't understand it.'

'They are all fuckers. All these kids.'

There was silence. I realized it was not a good idea to say that in front of Relentless who might die soon. I had to recover, like General Motors.

'Not Rashmi. I have given her a holiday to the US. Special prize.'

'Yes she is there now doctor. Leaving me alone. But I spoke to her. She's cut her holiday short—missing me—and is coming back.'

I was worried Relentless would start complaining about how I could let her daughter go to the US alone…blah blah…some crap. If only she knew what had happened.

'So you're a doctorate of something now is it Gupta?'

I could sense Tenzig's jealousy. It's bound to happen when life is unfair and makes one a hero and another a Bata salesman who disappeared into the 1980s midnight.

'This is my friend, Tenzig Chooha.'

'Hi. From London. Also Doctor. Dr Tenzig Chooha from London.'

'You are not the famous heart surgeon whose photo is on the cover of *The Times of India* this morning? You're here for a few days to receive a Padma Shri?'

'I am.'

So that's where the Chooha was hiding. Whatever. Awards aren't important. Some of the greatest business minds don't work for awards, they work for recognition. Two very different things. Remember. Read the Air India annual report. That airline is recognized by everyone, and its awards are zero.

People who fuck with your success are jealous

Rashmi's Air India return flight was detoured via New Zealand due to some unpaid fuel thing. And they charged me extra for it. I didn't want her to go to New Zealand because, I mean, who is she? John Wright? I wanted her back in the office. But there you have it—Air Crap, not Air India. That's my term by the way. So when she walked into office, late, I was ready.

'You're late, chanachoor.'

'Sir, they lost my bags.'

'Why are you holding…a monkey?'

'This is some other passenger's soft toy. There was some confusion. They told me they are trying—'

'Of course, no problem. I am compassionate. Just tell Bhola in Finance that you came in at 11 pm today, so that he'll adjust your pay, okay. Unimportant detail. Since that's settled, tell me, how are you?'

'Sir, I…I can't sleep at night after what I saw…'

'Yes, yes, one minute he's there, next minute… *poosh*. Pile of broken bones, smashed head.'

'Sir, I don't want to think of it. It was horrible—'

'Body parts everywhere...blood...*eeughh*...'

'Sir—'

'I just want to say that what you did was brave. Really brave. I have many employees here but what you did, really. And what are the chances? One in a million? You and the client next to each other? It was messed up, negro.'

'Sir, I did my best to save him.'

'Yeah, well, chiksaw, I don't mean the call itself because that, as we all know, was let's just say, not one of your best calls.'

Thought I would relax the tension with my subtle wit.

'Anyone would have done what I did in that situation.'

'Yeah, maybe. Fuck "anyone" though; that's too many people, it's not specific enough. You know what is? You. I didn't give anyone my pole, I gave *you* my pole. And the thing about you, chipaqua, is that you work for me. I gave you a pole that I used to love, caress, and dance around. Do you know why? It's because I thought you were someone who would take that pole from me and make it even taller. You would be on top, pole under you. A winner. I was even going to teach you how to eat sushi. Now if we look at your performance curve since you, well, killed Osama, it's moving downward...because instead of saying something to him, you just watched. After all that training to speak, you didn't speak. This is a business where the asset is words, not silence. This is not a silent business. Now that's a bit of a cause of concern isn't it? Actually, I'd say it's total fucking shit. Absolute total complete fucking rubbish. And I would hit you if this was Saudi Arabia. If you worked in outsourcing in the Middle Ages, they would burn you at the stake but this isn't and I am a patient man. I have studied history. You know what they would do to you at TCS? It's too embarrassing to even say. Out of your two main calls, you won one, Grocery Terence, negotiated with me for a 5,321 percent pay raise and now failed in one. That's a failure rate of what would you say?'

'50 percent, sir.'

'We have two people here. You're the worst performer of two people and you were my best. Now that is what? Not a perfect career advance wouldn't you say? In fact, I would say, it's the exact opposite of that. It is a 100 percent decline in your worth, that's what I would say. And you cost 5,321 percent more than Ramesh. So my total loss with you is 5,421 percent. That's the thing. And all the bills from Air India haven't even come in.'

'Maybe I start by taking the day off, sir.'

'You kids here think I'm busy at Blue Frog Bar fucking consulate chicks but in fact, I hear everything. More than God or wire-tapping. There are some things that even the media don't hear and they call me to ask. They call and say, "Hello Arun, what's going on? Tell us what's happening?" And I say, "I won't tell you, I won't reveal." If you take the day off, I know what will happen next—you will come late, then you won't come, then you'll lie about the number of calls you make. Young people think that we don't know dishonesty? How do you think I built businesses in the eighties? That's why now, at 1-888, it's all tracked. In PeopleSoft, I record it—then I record it in my head. You know all this?'

Actually, we didn't have a PeopleSoft call recording device because the fuckers charge $15,000 US plus maintenance so I only recorded the calls in my head. I was PeopleSoft. That's all you need really, memory; that's what PeopleSoft is, and I have that. It's not a good idea to say that to an employee you are giving a pep talk to though. They need to know they are being tracked by a machine, like a twenty-four by seven surveillance camera of their voice.

To be honest, I would have preferred PeopleSoft, I even tried to bribe the dealer but he said there was no point because the Korean manufacturers say the machine costs what it costs. I would never hear things like this in the eighties. The country is really going to hell. No business ethics.

'Sir, given what happened, a person needs time to recover. It's only human.'

'Chick, no more…you may think I wanted to do this one-on-one session to understand what went wrong, to give you space to vent your psychological fears, to really find out if you're still emotionally unwell? Does the "event" still cause mental shocks stressing out your day-to-day life? Do you need therapy? Are you physically capable? In America, it's called post-traumatic stress. You may think that's why we are having this meeting. But I DON'T GIVE A FUCK ABOUT THAT. AND I DON'T GIVE A FUCK ABOUT YOU. THERE ARE PEOPLE WHO NEEDED TO BE SAVED AND YOU FAILED THEM. YOU FAILED ME. YOU PIECE OF LOWER-MIDDLE CLASS UNTOUCHABLE WADALA SHIT. AUNTY…AUNTY…'

In business, sometimes you have to fire people. That doesn't mean throwing them out. It means abusing them in a manner that will insult them and make them feel worthless. You could also throw something at them. David Ogilvy, the ad guru, went even further—he sometimes threw people out of a window of his Manhattan office if they lost an account. But he got ambulances and such to heal them back up. Then get back on the ground managing clients. That's what business is about—second chances. Being able to fall and get up again. Another example is the Hollywood agent Ari Emmanuel on whom a TV show called *Entourage* is based. Now some people think it's a comedy but I don't see it as funny, I see it as a business guide. Mr Emmanuel, through his leadership, shouts at people, brings up their sexual intercourse history, medical incapability history, family history, educational history, everything, so he can embarrass them in public. You have to. How else do you give a proper assessment when someone has veered in their company performance? It's like tearing up a person's resume every day in their face and then doing it again the next day. Yes, there is wastage of paper but look at the learning curve.

Whatever exercise you choose, make sure they feel the least amount of self-worth they will ever feel, so the only way from here is up. Bringing up a painful memory like a dead parent, or an exam where they lost something by one point, or being overlooked for a promotion they really wanted because of a deep insecurity—these are good tools. Here I targeted her economic background and her touchability status. All nerves that can be touched. Make sure it's a weak nerve though. In chess, this move is known as check.

Rashmi had played her moves by smuggling a holiday to the US out of me, became too big for her new Millionaire clothes. I played my move, checked her at my check point—threat followed by shouting followed by action. As the great US director Quentin Tarantino says, 'Bang Bang Bang'.

I pointed behind Rashmi. That was my set up. Rashmi's mother (Relentless Aunty) was standing there. Why? I had made her stand there. How? I brought her to the office and when in the office, I told her, 'When I point to you, stand there'. If you are a world expert as I am, you would know what this is in movie terms. For those who don't watch Hollywood (start), this is known as 'entering on cue'. Bollywood doesn't do that because none of the fuckers here enter at all and are atleast five hours late. But Spiderman enters on cue, he jumps into a den of villains. Aunty entered on cue because Bhola picked her up in an auto two hours earlier.

'Mama?'

'Your mother has something to say to you.'

'What are you doing here?'

'Aunty, come here.'

'I met a wonderful man my age.'

'My Mizo friend Tenzig Chooha.'

'He is in my pole dancing class.'

'Aunty, tell her what's happened.'

'Last night he asked me if I wanted to live with him in London. I really love him. But he has grown-up kids in the UK, he's divorced but they stay with him and you know how it is there. But he said if you wanted to, you could visit anytime, there would be a room for you. It's the first time I've ever found something that I really want to do since your father died. Some genuine happiness. We met the day you left and he calls me every hour since. Sends flowers. Won't it be incredible to go live in London for a while? And you don't like me annoying you all the time, you are grown up now. I don't like fighting with you about a pole, this job, you eating on time, this that. You have your life. And I have a chance to have this. Then you're here and I've never left you alone. What do you think a mother should do? Give up on something so perfect or carry on living like this?'

'Why are you telling me this here? What is going on? Why didn't you tell me earlier?'

'Arun said he was like a parent to you. He said I come to office and tell you.'

'We had a one-on-one, heart-to-heart tête-à-tête, right, aunty?'

'Yes.'

'So what should she do, Rashmi?'

'What should I do?'

'You should go,' said Rashmi quietly.

'See, aunty, I knew she loves you. Now will you give us five minutes aunty? Office work?'

'Okay.'

'LEAVE AUNTY!'

'Okay.' And with that the mother left me to close the deal with Rashmi.

'So you have to be all alone now. That is your punishment for fucking up. I told you, I, like God or Mahendra Singh Dhoni can give you a chance but I can also take it away. You did well, I gave you New York. I said here's New York, take it. You fucked up, you lost your mother. In Roman times, if you lost a war, you became a slave and they cut off your arm. Here it's mother bye bye.'

People later accused me of being some crazy person. Someone even said on rediff.com that I was like that German man, the doer I mentioned earlier, who had chained his family for thirty years in a basement jail. Antara sent me that link. Point is that they don't understand business. In fact most common people don't, so they pass judgement, jump to conclusions. Especially you, raghavstud45@rediffmail.com. I mean, do you even know what ROI is?

Look, what happened between aunty and Chooha has nothing to do with me. As you witnessed, I only introduced them. What is business if not networking? I networked them to each other. But I had no idea it would be romantic. When aunty came to me with the news, it was like coming to me with the Coca Cola formula. I had to say whoa. And Rashmi was away on some roof in New Jersey recovering from having watched a suicide, so I thought, why tell her then. Best to surprise her now. Use it carefully as a live example in my motivational lecture and HR pep talk to her. Some people use PowerPoint, to explain things to a room of employees. Fuck PowerPoint, I said. I had aunty. Human is better than font, that's what I say.

The important lesson here is on information. As a boss, when you are given information, that aunty loves Chooha and you know Rashmi doesn't know, what do you do with it? If it's valuable information, how do you monetize it? If it's secret or confidential information, how do you keep it from competitors and use it to compete with them? Lots of businesses are entirely built around how to manage information. They do it so much that they become information businesses. Look at the CIA or Reuters.

On a separate note, how can anyone love Chooha? He is uglier than most Sri Lankan fast bowlers.

My goal here was not to use this information to separate families. No. That's the job of TV soap operas. I just wanted to use it to get better business results by navigating the right speech and therefore, the mind of my employee.

I don't believe in mind mapping by the way. I don't even know what that is. I do believe in mind bending though. I should be able to bend an employee's mind in any direction and she should not be able to tell where I'm driving. That's what I was doing and it's what I do. Like David Blaine. A mind magician. There is no space to talk about him in this book but he is important for business because he is there—also in London—and does what he does.

Returning to the moment. I had a surprise up my sleeve for Rashmi. In fashion, a surprise is known as the showstopper because the show stops to look at it (whatever it is). In Karan Johar's (another American) TV show, the showstopper is sometimes a surprise guest. Here, it was time to stop the show and bring it out.

'But then I think, you were my Top Gun, you were my cheerios, how can I let this happen? I'm not totally heartless like Stalin or *The Economist*. Sudha?'

'Who is this?'

'Sudha. Sudha, say hi to Rashmi.'

'Hello, madam.'

'Rashmi, Sudha is my present to you.'

'I don't understand.'

'Sudha is a woman. She has no children. You lost your mother. In business terms, it's a perfect fit.'

'What?'

'She is your new mother. She is on an eight-hour shift plus overtime and don't worry, I'm paying, so you can do whatever mother–daughter things you want. Shopping, gossip, whatever.'

'Are you saying…?'

'Yes, I have outsourced your mother to Sudha. She has no training but she will pick up skills as she goes along.'

'Sir, I don't need a new mother.'

'Are you sure?'

'Yes.'

'It's a shame. Okay, Sudha, you can go.'

'But, sir, you said—'

'Fuck off please.'

Sudha left.

'Sir, I would like to resign.'

'Ha ha ha…'

'I can't take this anymore.'

Okay, this I was not expecting. Honestly, employees nowadays have no dedication. All I was trying to do was to motivate her to not make the same mistake again. That's all. If this was Bharat Heavy Metal and we were in the middle of Dhanbad and the same thing had happened, do you think the assistant plant manager could resign just like that? Just because she felt like it? This is the problem with new India—everything is too casual.

You know the carrot and the stick thing? It's an old negotiation technique that people at Sony used to use. You give the opponent a carrot and if they don't eat it, beat them with a stick. The carrot is a consolation prize, a truce thing. That's how they bought Universal Studios in Hollywood. I always wondered how the carrot worked for the Japanese because they eat fish and the US guys eat steak. So how did they sign a three-billion deal with a carrot? Honestly, sometimes people surprise you. Sudha was my carrot for Rashmi. She didn't eat it. Now the stick had to come out.

'You really want to do that? Do you know what I will do to you? Ramesh! RAMESH!'

'Sir?'

'Rashmi is leaving 1-888. Do you have anything you want to say to her?'

'Arun sir told me to take photos when we were practising with his USB. If you resign, I will have to put it on Facebook.'

Simple, one-word theory really—surveillance. At Sun or Oracle or Microsoft, they have surveillance to make sure you are not stealing the source code of the software. Photos and eye scan. Here, I take the same idea and reverse it. Surveillance photos of my employees humping. And it's not spying. Ramesh took some of himself naked also. Both are stored in my USB. Just in case. Like I said, personal and professional equals professional. Now you may say, Arun, that's personal, that's a breach of privacy. That's what the CBI later said. And the *Indian Express*. But whatever. Do you think they would have caught those terrorists on 26/11 without tapes? What about those other terrorists who tried to blow up Heathrow? It was taped in their homes while they made bombs and ate biryani. Homes are private. Without private camera photos, how would we ever know that Pamela Anderson is into sex? Or for that matter, Britney Spears. It's all thanks to photos.

But I had no real plans to put naked pictures of Rashmi on the Internet. That's the thing with a stick. It cannot kill people. It's a threat. I just didn't want her to go. The way she handled that bathtub drowning software guy in New York, I could see her becoming a future Indra Nooyi but I could not tell her that directly. That would be the wrong way to get her to stay. This was better. She had had a mental shock. I needed to shock the shock out of her so we could get the old Rashmi back. Whole Osama forgotten. USA holiday gone. And then there would be no stopping her, like ET's flying bicycle, a billion dollars' worth of saves. I could see it. I would even give her stock options if we listed on the NYSE. That's my main skill in business. Seeing what might happen, now and forever. I wouldn't call myself the Nostradamus of outsourced suicide hotlines, that's for other people to say.

And people management. I know psyches. What someone is thinking when.

'As I explained to him, if you did not work here, I see no point in helping your reputation. There are plenty of chicks in the sea...of chicks. This one...it's okay if we let her drown online under the weight of some dirty photos. I meant you. What do you have to say, Ramesh?'

'Yes, sir.'

'But, sir, you told me to have sex with Ramesh because you said he liked me and wanted to marry me. You said you wanted us to get engaged.'

'I did but look at Henry the Eighth. He was engaged eight times. That's why the name. But did he marry once? No. Why? He was probably getting a promotion at 1-888.'

There was silence. I could sense victory.

'Arun sir, I'm sorry.'

Victory. My strategies are much more than that really. They are tactics. The rate of success I have manipulating people, I should not limit my strategies to business, it should be expanded to war, philanthropy, video game design, furniture design, religion maybe, who knows. I should think about patents for each.

'We all make mistakes. I accept biatch.'

'Sir, I'd like to touch your feet.'

'Yes. Respect. Ramesh, learn from this example. I knew you were smart. The thing is, like Chinese chequers, you need to know where you belong. You belong here. And you can't go anywhere else. Now look at Ramesh. You know how rubbish he was. And then he became Scarlett so now I will pay for his sister's wedding or abortion or whatever. See, that's how it works. It's all performance-based performance. Today you have to bend over but when you improve, I will again reward you.'

Now some may look at what happened next as Rashmi hitting me in the balls, but I look at it as something bigger. As Shakespeare said to Julius Caesar, 'Et Tu Betrayal'. It's like that (no I'm not showing off about how much history I've read but as you can see, I have). Point is, there was mutual trust—that's the basis of any business. When I hire someone to be the head of my product management team, I assume they will manage the product. I don't assume they will hit me in my balls. So when I allowed Rashmi permission to touch my feet, there was an implicit understanding that she would do that. That's what gave me the confidence to relax my pelvis area if you will, ease my genitals. Knowing she was heading lower. So you can imagine my surprise when the blow came. And imagine the surprise for my balls and penis. It's like being in World Trade Center Tower 1, working for a fixed income trading firm, where one second you are tracking your bond prices, and the next minute watching a jet coming towards you. Same thing here. And yes, I will say this in public. In many ways, Rashmi was my 9/11. Actually, in all ways. After that 9/11 balls thing, the world changed. For me.

She did some other things also that I will describe I guess in one word as vandalism. She hit me with a shoe. She threw a chair at Ramesh. She screamed out things that I cannot describe as words. Yes, Prestige Business Centre's chair, which Longines would definitely bill to me. There was a movie in my USB,

Tarzan Fucks, maybe she saw that and got carried away. I have read about double-crossing before. I heard a rumour that a VP of marketing at Disney wanted to steal three Disney characters and run away, claiming the franchise as his. I have seen people urinating at the Shipping Corporation of India's Annual General Meeting, unhappy with the share price. I have heard of people stealing inventory—it happened to Hilton Hotels (their vegetable supply was 13 percent short), where someone was stealing babycorn. I have never, however, heard a great business story about an employee hitting a boss in the balls. Readers, I don't know what lesson to leave you with here. Except, if you plan to hire someone, buy an abdomen guard.

Yes, I am a believer in the American employee review system of feedback from colleagues above and below you. I encourage open discussion and disagreement on strategy, as you saw earlier from me giving Ramesh a beating. I even think that under extreme circumstances, like paralysis or coma, you should allow a productive and trustworthy person to work from home. Some firms call it 360-degree feedback, but I call it 360-degree feedback. You get a 360-degree view of yourself as an employee, like a room with only mirrors. If you aren't following me, go to Phuket.

I have never, however, believed in violence as a next step after a free and frank discussion with workers. Some may think this but I don't think it helps you get a promotion. Yes it shows initiative but that initiative can work against you if you end up in jail. It's true I didn't go to the police about Rashmi because of my other customs…anyway, the point is that I didn't complain to the police but if I had, her initiative would have turned into prison sentence. And prison doesn't look good on the CV. Imagine if it's said work experience—BPO Hanes, BPO 1888, then Arthur Road Jail. Not a climbing career is it?

If she had maturity, this should have been seen as an everyday business issue, a pep talk. Okay, because it's got mother and feelings involved, at worst, an internal small issue like workplace happiness imbalance. Human resource would categorize that as 'employee unhappiness'. We could have talked. How can that have been resolved by a kick in the balls at a *Fortune 500*? Maybe other experienced managers know more. Maybe at Ford or GM or other industries in decline, these things are forgiven. I once heard a TATA Steel story about someone pushing their manager into a furnace by accident. But that was an accident. And it was Patna. He didn't throw him into a furnace over some tiny thing like your mother running away with a Mizo pole dancer.

I wanted to say many things but I was almost passed out holding my balls, which, at that point in time, needed me. Like the airline industry needs government bailouts. Even though I was down, I was leading like Hank Paulson of the US Treasury during the US financial crisis.

I imagined how female CEOs wouldn't find themselves in this crisis. Advantage women. I always suspected genital ceiling would someday backfire against men.

All I did end up saying was, 'Woman, GIVE ME MY POLE BACK!'

There have been many great walk-outs in the history of business. Paul Allen, Steve Jobs, and Bill Gates went their separate ways. The founder of Facebook and other people who claimed they started it headed in different directions and ended up in court. Boardroom power struggles often result in someone resigning, like the HSBC chairman. The CEO of Morgan Stanley lost the CEO position in a backstabbing. He walked into a Manhattan street with no testicle injury. Never, however, is anyone found on the floor of their office holding their balls. I was.

That's the thing about a corporate 9/11, you can't see it coming and it's hard to get up. In the real 9/11 you didn't have to. You just died. Here, you were left behind, balls in hand, chair on head, one employee staring at you, defeated. You knew your competition was not like you. You know at 24/7 or WNS, there they were, in Gurgaon, standing straight, staring from the glass office above at the sea of BPO youth, balls intact. Fuck you competition, once I put some ice, I'll be back.

Not behind, sideways, or under, looking ahead

First things first. I want to clear up a few misconceptions. I'm not hiding in London. I don't hide. I'm not a hider, I am a leader. Indian Telecom ministers hide. Shady Karol Bagh lobbyists cutting deals with shady bureaucrats hide. I shop at Marks and Spencer, which, if you don't know London, is in the public. Clearly, when I am buying chicken bhuna in their basement takeout, people can see me.

Yes, I know what the CBI is. I know what a raid is. I know what the Department of Company Affairs is and the rules of the Ministry of Finance. No, it's not that I wasn't officially registered as a company—Bhola had the notarized papers and was going to drop them off. He just didn't get the time. And what do they mean I can't hire employees under the Employee Protection Act? I am paying, so I can hire. So what if 1-888 is not officially recognized by some stupid ministry? Do you think when the British built their tea gardens they asked the Company Law Board? How could they? The tea gardens were in Assam, Company

Board was in Delhi, no cell phones—you do the math. Did anyone charge Goodricke of torture or violation of Indian corporate law? I am not saying that was the charge against me but I'm just saying. Tea still became a billion-dollar industry.

By the way, there are no charges. Rashmi's case was pointless and flimsy. What was the case even about? That I was a demanding boss? Wake up, negro. Look at Infosys or TCS or Birla Sunlife's sales targets. You think that comes without life and death? And in our case, it was literally life and death. Save death equals to better life. How much clearer could I have been? There is something hugely wrong with a nation that a little whiny teenage girl's complaint is referred to the Ministry of Finance and SEBI and all that crap. This is why no one wants to do business with India. This is why those dying clients would rather die than talk to someone here, despite what I tried to do to prove that 1-888 was a phone line over there. This is why, generally, the West is better than over here, I mean India. This is why the Sensex falls eight hundred points sometimes and Laxmi Mittal lives in London. Yes, we're growing at 8 percent but what does it take to decline at 8 percent? One girl with her mother in a police station saying a CEO bugged her. That's it. Next thing you know, the Nano is being built in Algeria. Next thing you know, Arun Gupta, applicant to the prestigious Wolverhampton School of Business, almost honorary doctorate of Lovely Professional University, recipient of Harvard

Business School's Cease and Desist letter, is a fraud and an absconder.

I know what 'charges' are. I went to Hansraj College for God's sake. What do you think we did there for three years? That hockey stick Maruti gypsy ragging incident was only five days in jail. That still left me with two years and 360 days of learning time. I learnt Indian corporate laws. I was taught. It's called civics. Children know this. If Professor Das wasn't dead, you could have asked him.

And no, Bombay High Court did not file any torture charges against me. Just fraud. None that were ever sent to me anyway. And I strongly protest against the Internet blogs that said that I had destroyed the careers of young people. Fuck you @govindC++. You didn't work for me, you don't know. Who are you anyway? Claiming to be a software employee protection blog. I'm not even a software company. I fall under telecom.

The point is that I'm not scared. Did Rashmi leave and go and tell the Powai police station that I am a criminal? Yes. Did the CBI and Income Tax department of Maharashtra raid the business centre? Maybe. Depends on whom you believe—*The Economic Times*, *Business Standard*, *rediff.com*, and *Hindustan Times*, or Bhola. I can see your choice will be as obvious as mine—the latter. You've probably never heard of those publications whereas Bhola you met in this book. You know he cooks, knows Microsoft Excel, and is trustworthy. Familiarity is everything in business; ask any wine producing company that. Go ask Sula.

And as another great man, Lalit Modi, said to me at a Starbucks in Piccadilly Circus, 'Fuck the media'. Well, not exactly to me, to Javed Miandad (another leader) but I was listening. What do the media know anyway, except for reporting what happens? Anyone can do that. What kind of a headline is 'CEO of Outsourcing Company Harasses Employee's Mother'? I didn't harass her. I didn't say, 'Here is a pole, aunty, get on it. There is Tenzig, go hump him.' Things happened. Apparently, some TV channel said, 'CEO Running Sweatshop Absconding'. First of all, if I am running a sweat shop like the Chinese, where are the clothes? Second, if I am absconding, how come my brother and my sister-in-law know that I am staying with them in Wimbledon?

I like Lalit. We're quite alike, him and I. We tried to build a dream, a great grand extravaganza of wealth and might in a country not ready for it. Imagine explaining to the Egyptian pharaohs that going to the moon is possible or to the Roman Empire that you can have a building like the Burj Al Arab. It's a timing thing, and Lalit and I are ahead of it. Am I like the IPL of outsourcing? Without a question, yes. So why does IPL get 154 million hits on Google and 1888 Dial India only five? Essentially because Lalit had a captive audience of four million and I had a little bit less. And stadiums always draw bigger crowds than phones. Plus, at the end of a 20-20 game, everyone lives, so the numbers stay the same but in a suicide hotline, you lose someone sometimes, so the audience reduces. Anyway, the point is, I think I need to go over and have a cup of tea with him in Knightsbridge. I tried last week and if those security guards or whatever hadn't... Anyway, it's a matter of time till we meet. Our minds have.

Everyone needs some time off. Arun Sarin said he wanted to leave Vodafone to spend more time with family. The CEO of *Hustler* said he wanted to spend some time not thinking about naked girls. So you see, everyone has a need to get away. That's what London is for me. And it helps that my brother and his wife give me a list of tasks to complete daily. The other day, this Pakistani limo driver said, 'Oh, you're just Mohit Gupta's servant, he makes you do all his errands.' And I could have snapped back at him saying, 'Go deal with your floods Pakistani man' but I didn't. He doesn't know that the toilet cleaning, picking up Rohena from school, taking her to tennis, changing Suhail's diapers, helping Ilena with the dusting, returning the DVD to Bollywood Castle, are all therapeutic activities. You know when James Cayne's company, Bear Stears, was collapsing, he was playing bridge. Not because he didn't care or that he was like a retired Parsi yacht owner, but because he was 3D—in other words, three dimensional. A Renaissance man.

And I'm not the only one. If you walk behind Harrods and toward Kensington, you'll find a series of mansions. Someone said the first one belongs to some Rwandan warlord, then a bunch of them to Pakistanis who often run away—Nawaz Sharif, Musharraf, Zardari, Imran Khan. One to a nice Bosnian guy called Slobodan something—looks like an intellectual—then the great Zimbabwean hero Robert Mugabe. Donald Trump has the last big one. And then there's a Burmese Junta General and Suresh Kalmadi. Kim II Jong has been looking for a while but can't seem to find one.

I often walk around and know how much I am like these people. Not walk around exactly because they have a remote control iron gate but see from the outside when I am coming back from diaper shopping. I stare but try to not to get late because Mohit's wife, the whore, locks the door on my face, which leaves me on the street where I have to sleep and... Anyway, these people, they've done incredibly great things. Everyone knows their names and sees them as important players in world power. If they all went back, they would get a hero's reception. Like them, I could be back in India being a leader of men, I could get on that London-Mumbai flight BA 141 like Sachin or Rittikk Roshshannn, but I choose to be here in London because I'm a Renaissance man.

Today, again, there was some rubbish Calcutta newspaper—*Telegraph*—story about my brother making me pay rent, and that I begged and cried for him to let me in. Let me tell you that that's not what happened. What do they know about my personal relationships? If their photographer got a photo that made me look like I was on my knees crying, it's because we hadn't seen each other in four months. We are emotional Punjabis, we cry and the younger brother falls. It's a ritual...what can I say? Read about culture, and definitely watch *Monsoon Wedding*, before you pass any judgment. Fucking Suprotim photographer. And financially, my brother and I have an arrangement. If you studied finance you would know that you cannot charge interest on rent. Mohit gives me some money on which he charges interest, from which I pay the loan. That's not rent. Fuck you Calcutta papers. This is why I don't like Bengalis. Always talking about families that are not theirs and meddling, and drinking tea. The only Bengali I like is Aparna Sen because she got wet in a movie I saw a little bit of, and yes, maybe I was a bit drunk that night because of Antara leaving. The point is, I like wet Bengalis. But definitely not the dry ones.

You know, in time, Rashmi will realize what she's done. Okay, maybe she won't but India definitely will. There is a book about business called *The Black Swan*. Read it. The author claims that sometimes a black swan shows up at your workplace and your business collapses because you wonder how a fucking black swan got into an office where everyone else is a person. There's no lake in your office. It's a once-in-a-lifetime event. Rashmi was my Black Swan. There is another book which I highly recommend called

Freakanomics. Appropriate for India. It's about what happens when freaks take over the economy. Freaks like Rashmi. Young, part of the seven hundred million power house fuelling India. We're not a 'developing economy', we're a 'freak economy'. People will realize that soon, you watch. Then everyone will end up living in their brother's spare Renault in a garage without heating. You watch.

Any new idea can only be done by dreamers. Do you think if you asked people that someday, a talking mouse would be a billion-dollar company, people would have let you stay outside an asylum? If you told Marco Polo he was an idiot for taking two years to go to China when you could do that in fourteen hours, he would have believed you? That's why outsourcing is in India. In the future—a future I will build, once I get out of this garage—everything will be outsourced, you see. Death is only a beginning. Work, holiday, love, emotions, funerals, food, money, masturbating, everything. And that day you will say, 'Shit, I now need to pay Arun Gupta $149.99 plus tax to manage my outsourced life when I could have paid him $9.99 plus tax.'

Without these dreams nothing would have happened, Sunil Mittal would not have built Airtel, he would still be trying to get his home phone fixed. Oberoi would not be a famous hotel, it would just be a surname. Ratan Tata's Nano would cost at least two lakhs and Lavasa would just be a coffee instead of India's most ambitious real estate project.

Without dreams, 1888 Dial India would have just been numbers on a page to be shown to a lady late for a midnight flight. Instead it is a list of the following successes. I like to look at these as five profits. Not every kind of profit needs to be deposited in a bank. Ask any Marwari.

1) A software employee cooking a meal for his family instead of dying in a bathtub.
2) A little girl finding her saviour in Scarlett Johansson.
3) An Indian girl being the first one in her family to visit the US.
4) A 25 year old paying for his sister's wedding. Actually, I paid for it. It was a lavish wedding in their house. Food from Dominoes man. Lavish. No, no guests. On Skype. I told Ramesh it's the digital age—no need to get married in person. It's uncool.
5) I signed Ramesh's letter of recommendation under the pseudonym Azim Premji. He now has a job as an Assistant Team Leader at Wipro. He sent me an email saying he will put a down-payment on something called Lakhotia Hercules. I think it's a gym. He's come a long way. And the point is that I made him.

You see what's happened here. What business has done. Not by filing papers with Company Boards, but by doing. That's what I do with money—I make dreams, I don't waste it in attempting to make more money. The real Azim Premji gives away a billion dollars but I am a different sort of philanthropist. I build a billion dreams and then give it away. Just like that catchy MasterCard ad I would say, 'Some things in life are priceless, like working for Arun Gupta. For everything else there is MasterCard'.

That's my motto too.

A brief encounter

Sometimes, from the garage, Mohit's wife lets me in upstairs to watch TV. I saw this movie by David Lean called *Brief Encounter.* Two people had a brief encounter. It gave me a business idea. Then I had my own brief encounter that changed everything. The movie was in black and white. My encounter happened while I was carrying eight bags of rice from Safeway. It was for Mohit's whore wife who was throwing some party for obese NRI housewives. Anyway, the party looked like a scene from a Gurinder Chadda film.

The BBC said *Brief Encounter* was a rom-com, as in a romantic comedy about things unsaid between two old lovers meeting again. My meeting was more of a rom-biz—things unsaid between a VC and their portfolio company. Like love but with stock options.

I was on Jeremyn Street, off Bond Street, when it had started to rain and I saw Sarah. She looked like she was in a hurry. She saw me first. I didn't try to explain the rice. Or the charges or why we had shut down. She knew.

AVC and the company are like lovers—when nothing is said, everything is said. Like Apple's stock price.

'Arun, I gave you forty fucking thousand dollars.'

'I took your forty thousand dollars and built the new India. And the new India has saved over two American lives just with phones and people skills, and that too from Bombay. We were growing at 50 percent.'

'What happened to my money?'

'Forget it. What I am here to announce today is the next frontier in a cut-throat global business landscape. What is the new "new" thing in outsourcing?'

She tried to walk around me—an old VC-financier tactic to throw you off. I put down the Safeway bags in front of her. It threw her off.

'"Love", Sarah. In today's BlackBerry-Facebook-Twitter-YouTube-MySpace generation, when a young person spends most of his or her waking hours on the Internet, is there any need to fall in love in person? US divorce rates are over 60 percent. Most of Europe is single, like you...'

Always make a pitch personal. I didn't know about Sarah's personal life but I went again with guts combined with probability. Bad looking, two BlackBerries, private equity women are generally working too hard, always travelling. Combine that with the knowledge that when a lot of hot UK women are single, the stats for ugly ones must be worse. See the things I combined here—instinct, country statistics, probability, deduction. A business brain is like renewable energy—nothing is ever thrown away. A business brain like mine is what you get when Sherlock Holmes's brain, Einstein's brain, Wikipedia's brain and Mr Ravindra Bhanot's (Head of Indian Statistical Institute) brain make love. Don't try it at home. A) You don't have this brain and B) Four-way sex is illegal in India.

Back to pitching to Sarah, who I am now convinced, is single and lonely, so I have the upper hand. Not upper hand in life (in life, ok, I am also single and maybe a little lonely), just in this pitch.

'So it's clear that "live" relationships don't work. Our numbers show that there are over three hundred million single, attractive, photogenic Indian men and women and over sixty million single Americans. That's almost a choice of almost four single people for every single American. The American consumer wins again. If this indeed is the next Google, do you want to say you missed the boat? Do you? If not, there's only one answer. India. Jai ho!'

I threw in a *Slumdog* reference to show my knowledge of recent popular culture. Yes it's a few years old now, but Rahman is still big. He sang at Davos.

And to make a point, I picked up the bags again and looked away in the direction of Leicester Square. Climax.

I knew the rice was totally spoilt. I knew I'd have to sleep on the street again but like Linux versus Windows, like Adidas versus Puma, it was me versus chance.

'What is the market potential?' Sarah asked.

And I was back.

Acknowledgements

To the entrepreneurs building new India, for your ambitions, your deceit, and your genius. Without your insane dreams, new India would be a boring place.

To Raell Padamsee for her brilliant vision, relentless enterprise, and tremendous show business chutzpah in bringing this story to life.

To Kunaal Roy Kapoor, for finding and becoming an Arun Gupta far better than the Arun Gupta on paper.

To Rahul Da Cunha, for his enduring mentorship, constant friendship, notes on the play, and an impossibly brilliant eye in knowing what makes a play work.

To Ashim Ahluwalia, whose film *John and Jane* was the definitive work on outsourcing in new India, for coming to see the play.

To the cast and crew of the play *1888 Dial India*, especially Sid, Ratna, Ashwin, Sophie, Faezeh, Prerna, Prarthna, Rakshanda, Craig, Hannah Lambert, Matt Daniels, Sid Cuotto, Shoko Kambara, for embracing this story and making it yours in ways that only your brilliance could.

To everyone at Random House, especially Chiki Sarkar, Milee Ashwarya, and Trisha Bora, my publishing trinity that kept me honest and encouraged me to improve my mediocrity daily.

To my wife, the better storyteller and the wiser one.

To my mother, my biggest and only fan.

To my in-laws for their constant enthusiasm for the arts. Knowing them lets me know that someone is watching.

And to Manish Acharya, who will live forever.

A note on the author

Anuvab Pal is an acclaimed playwright and screenplay writer. His screenplays include the award winning *The Loins of Punjab* and *The President is Coming*. His plays, which have been performed at numerous festivals, include *Chaos Theory*, *Fatwa*, *Paris and Life*, *Love*, and *ETIBDA*. Anuvab has also written for the acclaimed sitcoms *Frasier* and *Law and Order*. He currently lives and works in Mumbai.

A note on the author

Anuvab Pal is an acclaimed playwright and screenplay writer. His screenplays include the award winning *The Loins of Punjab* and *The President is Coming*. His plays, which have been performed at numerous festivals, include *Chaos Theory*, *Fatima*, *Ulta* and [illegible] and [illegible]. Anuvab has also written for the acclaimed sitcoms [illegible]. He currently lives and works in Mumbai.